P9-DDM-900

My Little Pony™

Adventures in Friendship

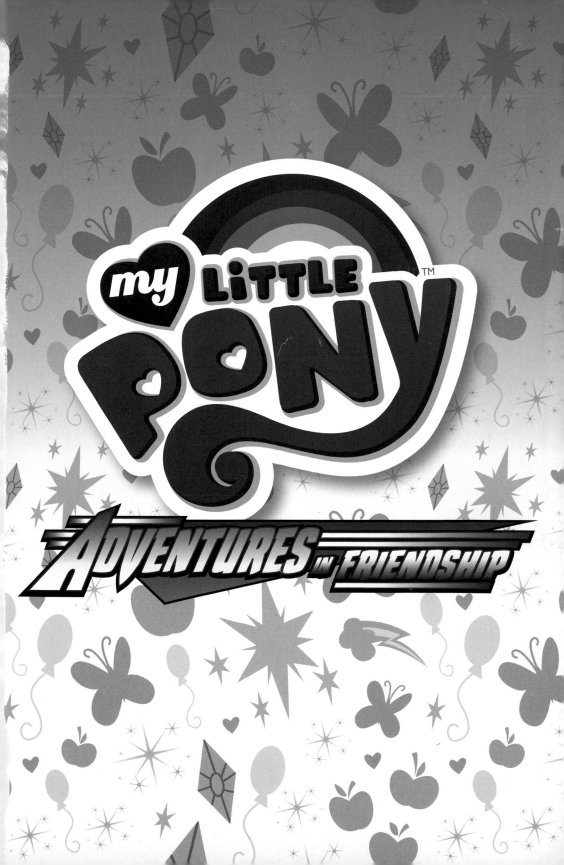

COVER BY SARA RICHARD
COLLECTION EDITS BY JUSTIN EISINGER AND ALONZO SIMON
COLLECTION DESIGN BY THOM ZAHLER

Special thanks to Erin Comella, Robert Fewkes, Joe Furfaro, Heather Hopkins, Pat Jarret, Ed Lane, Brian Lenard, Marissa Mansolillo, Donna Tobin, Michael Vogel, and Michael Kelly for their invaluable assistance.

ISBN: 978-1-63140-189-3

17 16 15 14   1 2 3 4

IDW
® Licensed By: Hasbro

www.IDWPUBLISHING.com

IDW founded by Ted Adams, Alex Garner, Kris Oprisko, and Robbie Robbins

Ted Adams, CEO & Publisher
Greg Goldstein, President & COO
Robbie Robbins, EVP/Sr. Graphic Artist
Chris Ryall, Chief Creative Officer/Editor-in-Chief
Matthew Ruzicka, CPA, Chief Financial Officer
Alan Payne, VP of Sales
Dirk Wood, VP of Marketing
Lorelei Bunjes, VP of Digital Services
Jeff Webber, VP of Digital Publishing & Business Development

Facebook: facebook.com/idwpublishing
Twitter: @idwpublishing
YouTube: youtube.com/idwpublishing
Instagram: instagram.com/idwpublishing
deviantART: idwpublishing.deviantart.com
Pinterest: pinterest.com/idwpublishing/idw-staff-faves

Originally published as MY LITTLE PONY MICRO-SERIES #2: RAINBOW DASH, MY LITTLE PONY MICRO-SERIES #4: FLUTTERSHY, and MY LITTLE PONY: FRIENDS FOREVER #6.

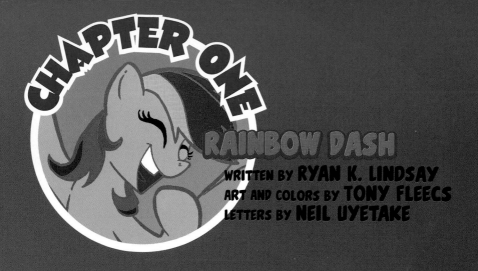

CHAPTER ONE

RAINBOW DASH

WRITTEN BY **RYAN K. LINDSAY**
ART AND COLORS BY **TONY FLEECS**
LETTERS BY **NEIL UYETAKE**

CHAPTER TWO

FLUTTERSHY

WRITTEN BY **BARBARA RANDALL KESEL**
ART AND COLORS BY **TONY FLEECS**
LETTERS BY **NEIL UYETAKE**

CHAPTER THREE

RAINBOW DASH AND TRIXIE

WRITTEN BY **THOM ZAHLER**
ART AND COLORS BY **AGNES GARBOWSKA**
LETTERS BY **NEIL UYETAKE**

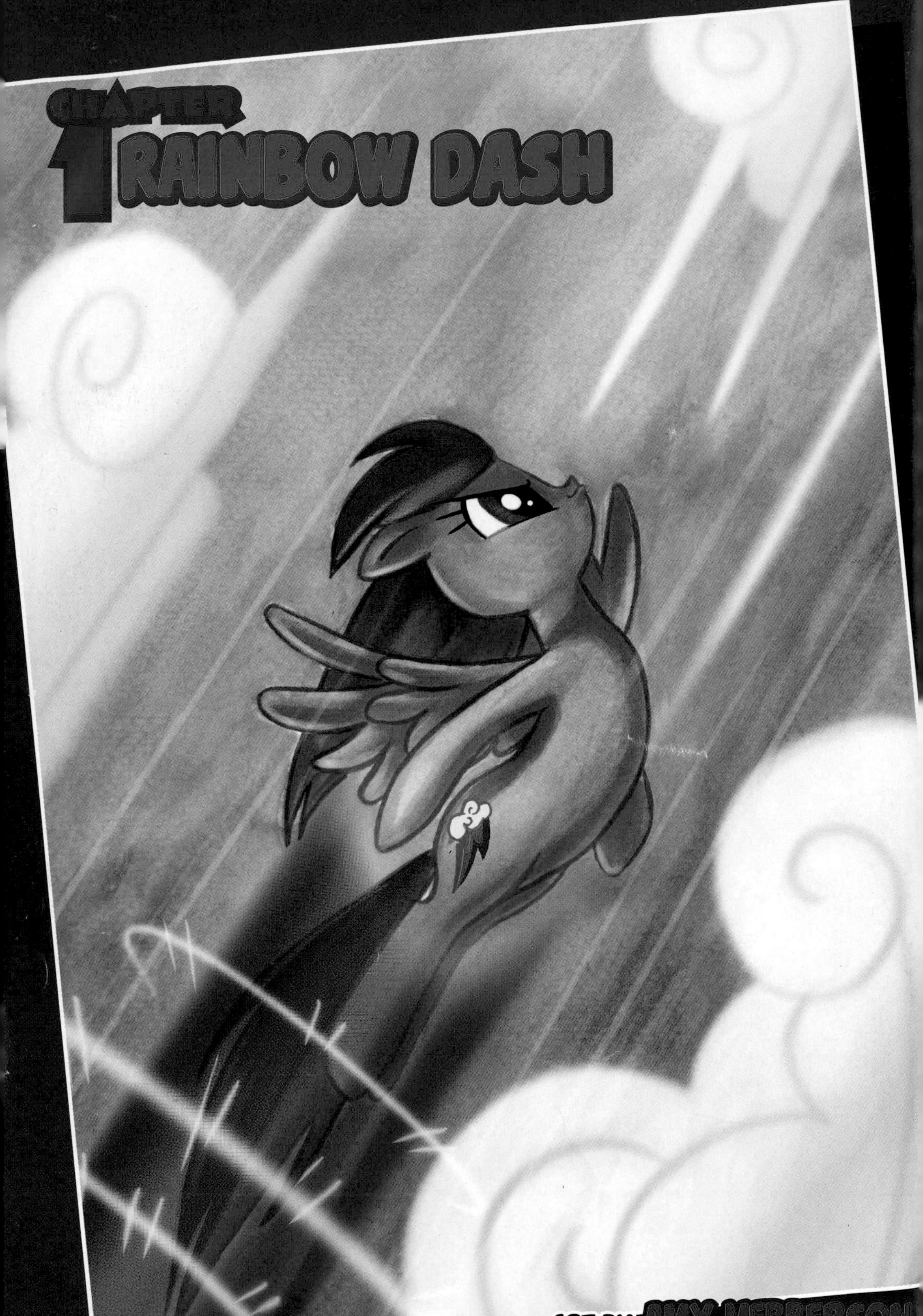
CHAPTER 1
RAINBOW DASH
ART BY AMY MEBBERSON

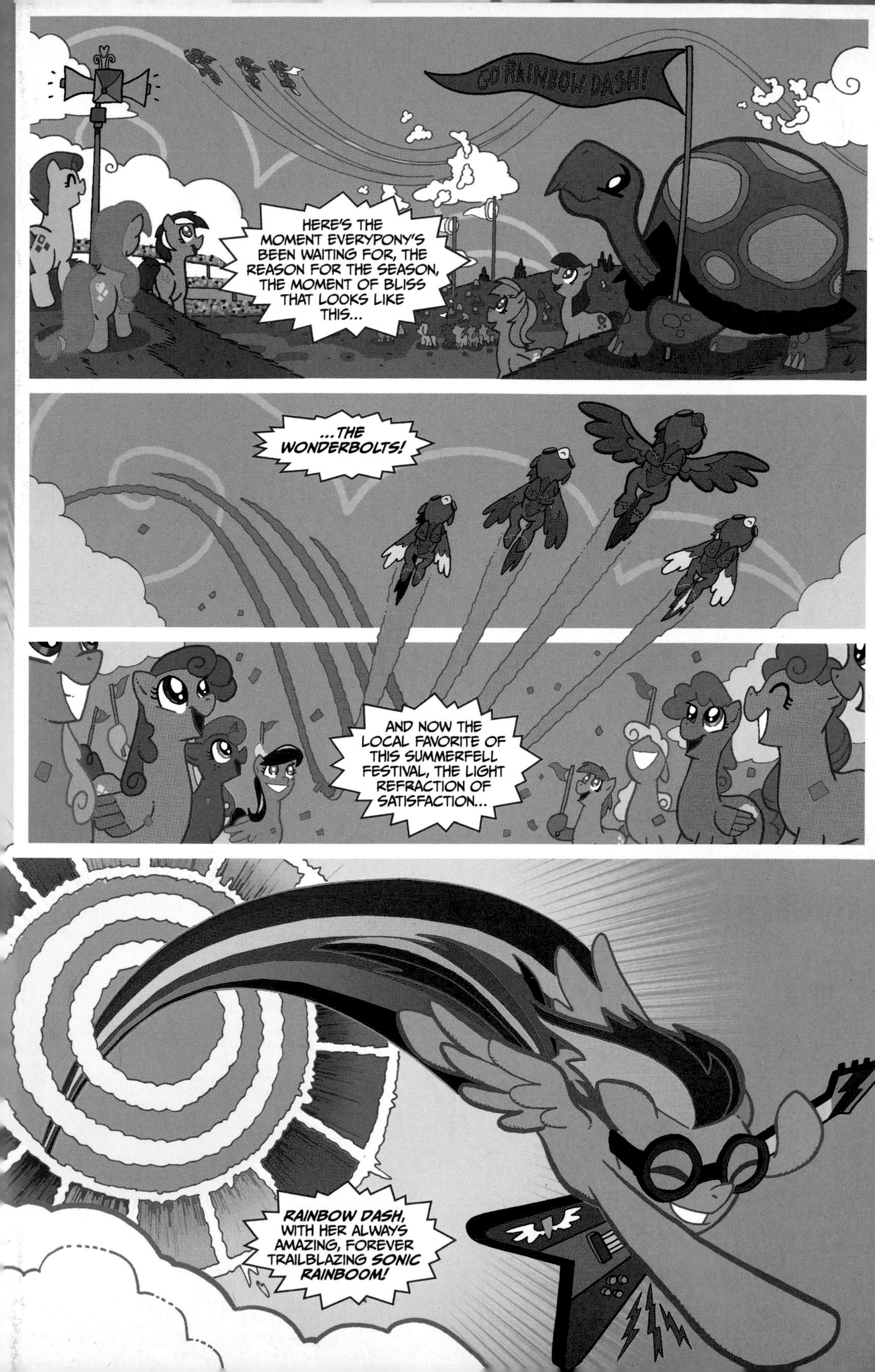
GO RAINBOW DASH!
HERE'S THE MOMENT EVERYPONY'S BEEN WAITING FOR, THE REASON FOR THE SEASON, THE MOMENT OF BLISS THAT LOOKS LIKE THIS...
...THE WONDERBOLTS!
AND NOW THE LOCAL FAVORITE OF THIS SUMMERFELL FESTIVAL, THE LIGHT REFRACTION OF SATISFACTION...
RAINBOW DASH, WITH HER ALWAYS AMAZING, FOREVER TRAILBLAZING SONIC RAINBOOM!

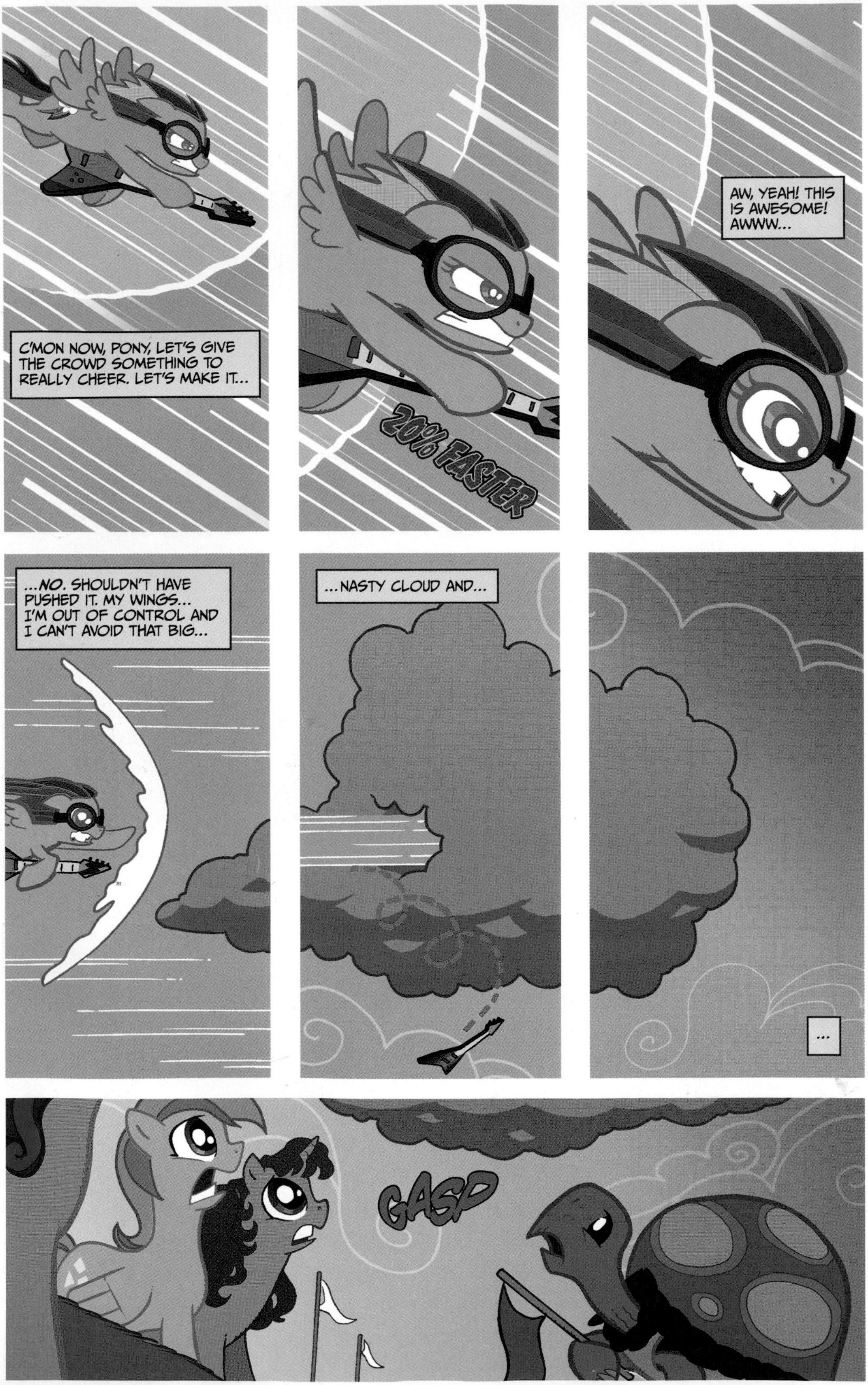

C'MON NOW, PONY, LET'S GIVE THE CROWD SOMETHING TO REALLY CHEER. LET'S MAKE IT...
20% FASTER
AW, YEAH! THIS IS AWESOME! AWWW...
...NO. SHOULDN'T HAVE PUSHED IT. MY WINGS... I'M OUT OF CONTROL AND I CAN'T AVOID THAT BIG...
...NASTY CLOUD AND...
...
GASP

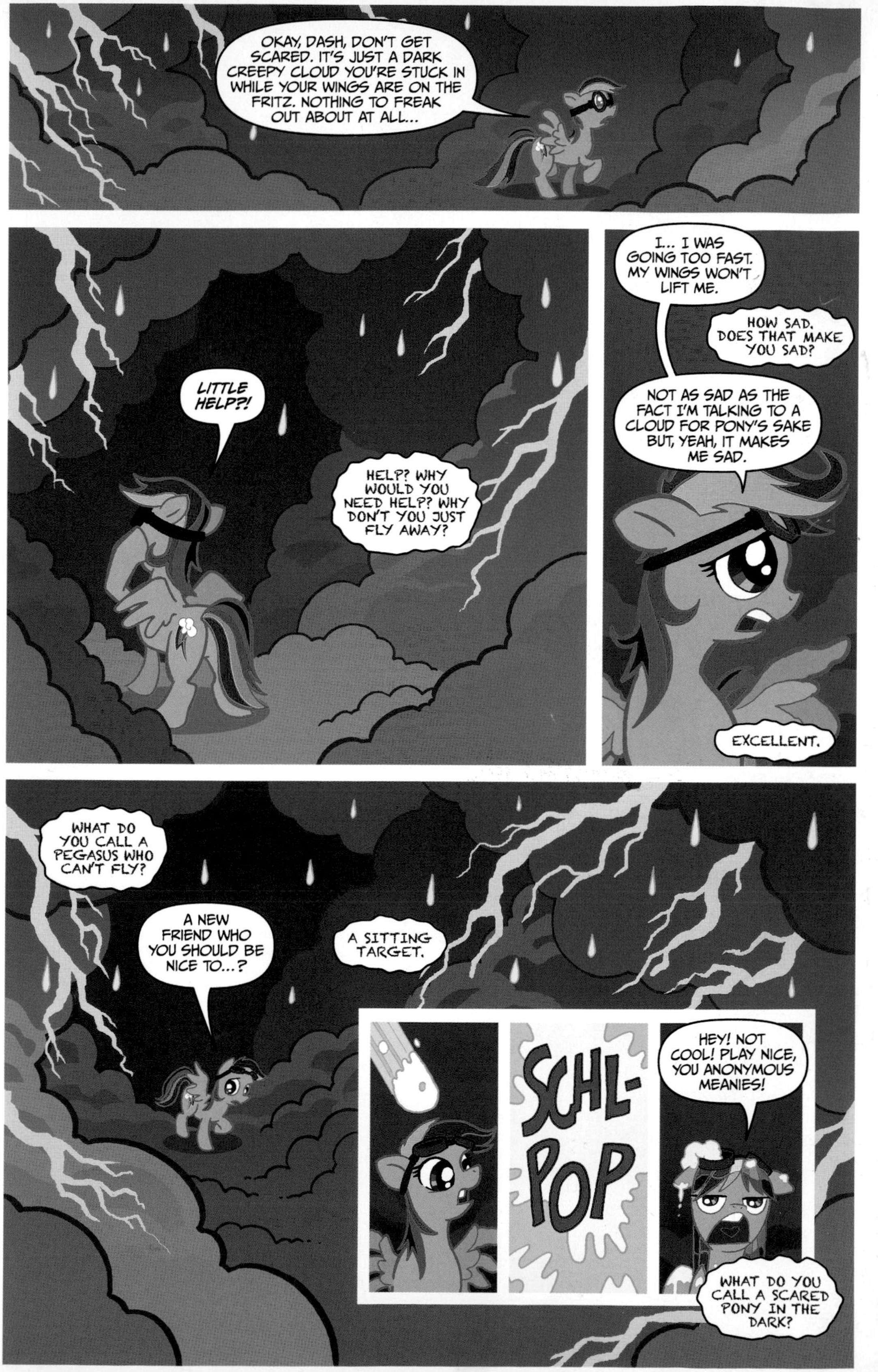
OKAY, DASH, DON'T GET SCARED. IT'S JUST A DARK CREEPY CLOUD YOU'RE STUCK IN WHILE YOUR WINGS ARE ON THE FRITZ. NOTHING TO FREAK OUT ABOUT AT ALL...
LITTLE HELP?!
HELP? WHY WOULD YOU NEED HELP? WHY DON'T YOU JUST FLY AWAY?
I... I WAS GOING TOO FAST. MY WINGS WON'T LIFT ME.
HOW SAD. DOES THAT MAKE YOU SAD?
NOT AS SAD AS THE FACT I'M TALKING TO A CLOUD FOR PONY'S SAKE BUT, YEAH, IT MAKES ME SAD.
EXCELLENT.
WHAT DO YOU CALL A PEGASUS WHO CAN'T FLY?
A NEW FRIEND WHO YOU SHOULD BE NICE TO...?
A SITTING TARGET.
SCHL-POP
HEY! NOT COOL! PLAY NICE, YOU ANONYMOUS MEANIES!
WHAT DO YOU CALL A SCARED PONY IN THE DARK?

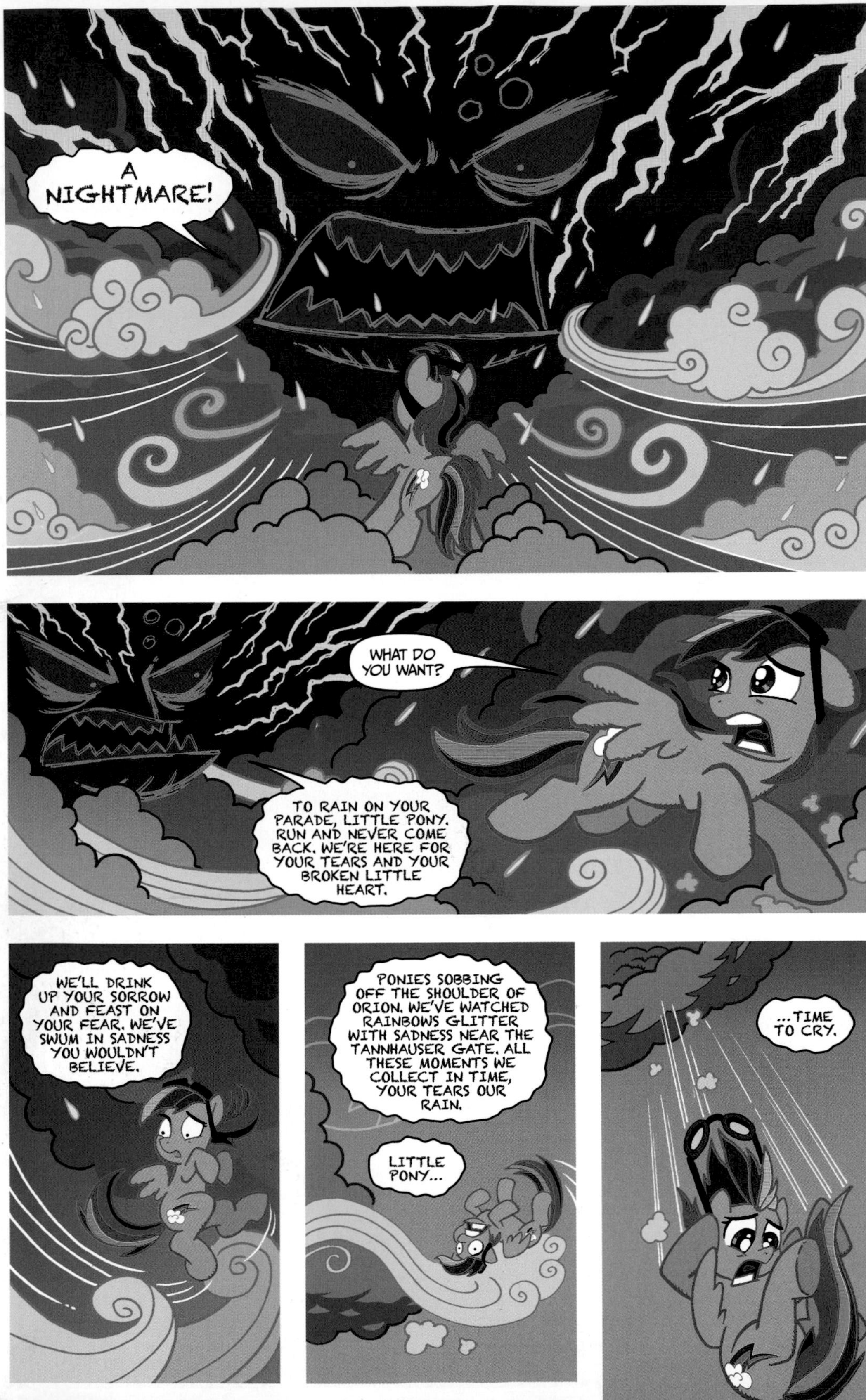
A NIGHTMARE!
WHAT DO YOU WANT?
TO RAIN ON YOUR PARADE, LITTLE PONY. RUN AND NEVER COME BACK. WE'RE HERE FOR YOUR TEARS AND YOUR BROKEN LITTLE HEART.
WE'LL DRINK UP YOUR SORROW AND FEAST ON YOUR FEAR. WE'VE SWUM IN SADNESS YOU WOULDN'T BELIEVE.
PONIES SOBBING OFF THE SHOULDER OF ORION. WE'VE WATCHED RAINBOWS GLITTER WITH SADNESS NEAR THE TANNHAUSER GATE. ALL THESE MOMENTS WE COLLECT IN TIME, YOUR TEARS OUR RAIN.
LITTLE PONY...
...TIME TO CRY.

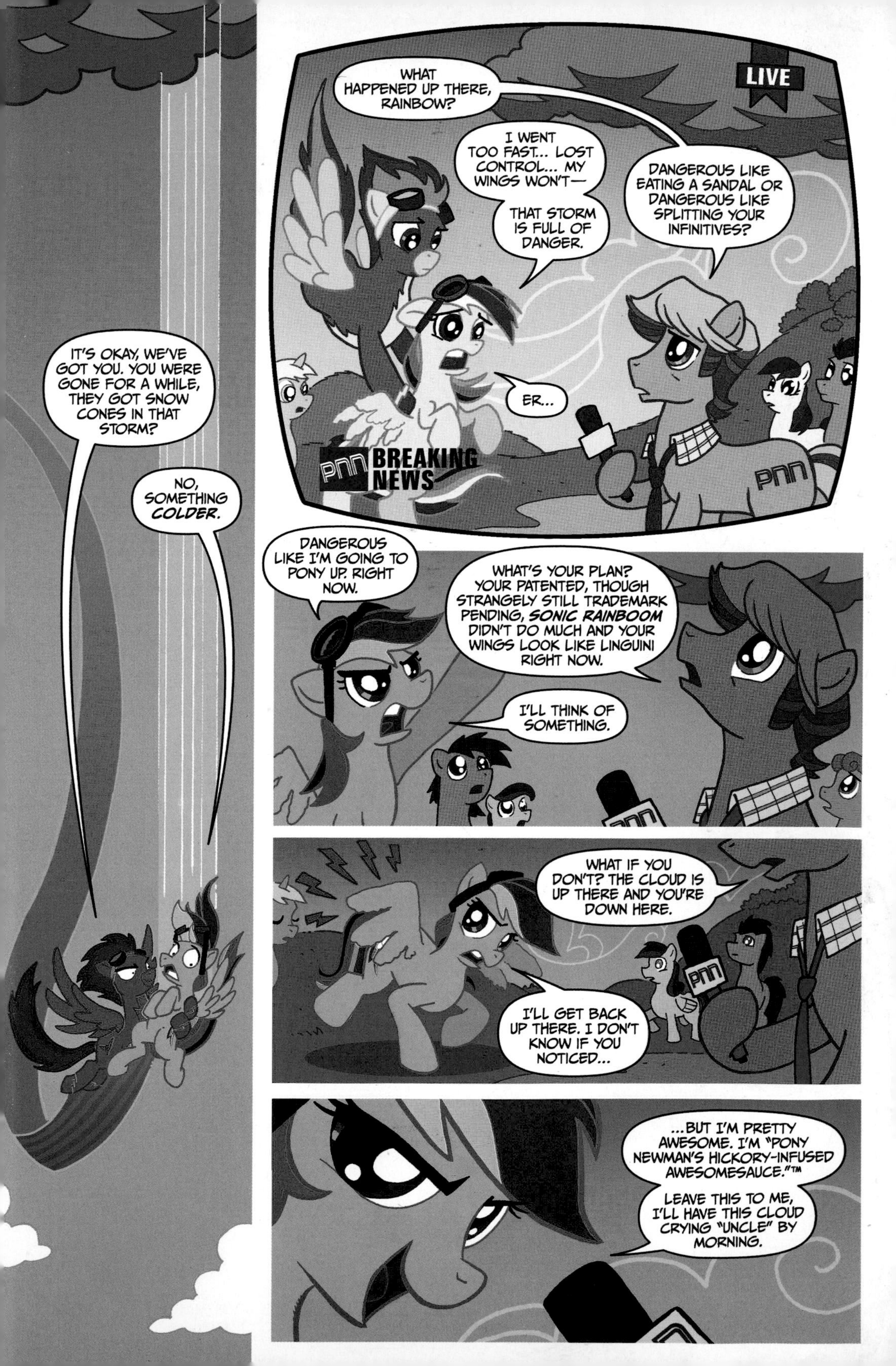

IT'S OKAY, WE'VE GOT YOU. YOU WERE GONE FOR A WHILE, THEY GOT SNOW CONES IN THAT STORM?
NO, SOMETHING *COLDER*.
LIVE
WHAT HAPPENED UP THERE, RAINBOW?
I WENT TOO FAST... LOST CONTROL... MY WINGS WON'T—
THAT STORM IS FULL OF DANGER.
DANGEROUS LIKE EATING A SANDAL OR DANGEROUS LIKE SPLITTING YOUR INFINITIVES?
ER...
PNN BREAKING NEWS
PNN
DANGEROUS LIKE I'M GOING TO PONY UP. RIGHT NOW.
WHAT'S YOUR PLAN? YOUR PATENTED, THOUGH STRANGELY STILL TRADEMARK PENDING, *SONIC RAINBOOM* DIDN'T DO MUCH AND YOUR WINGS LOOK LIKE LINGUINI RIGHT NOW.
I'LL THINK OF SOMETHING.
WHAT IF YOU DON'T? THE CLOUD IS UP THERE AND YOU'RE DOWN HERE.
I'LL GET BACK UP THERE. I DON'T KNOW IF YOU NOTICED...
...BUT I'M PRETTY AWESOME. I'M "PONY NEWMAN'S HICKORY-INFUSED AWESOMESAUCE."™
LEAVE THIS TO ME, I'LL HAVE THIS CLOUD CRYING "UNCLE" BY MORNING.

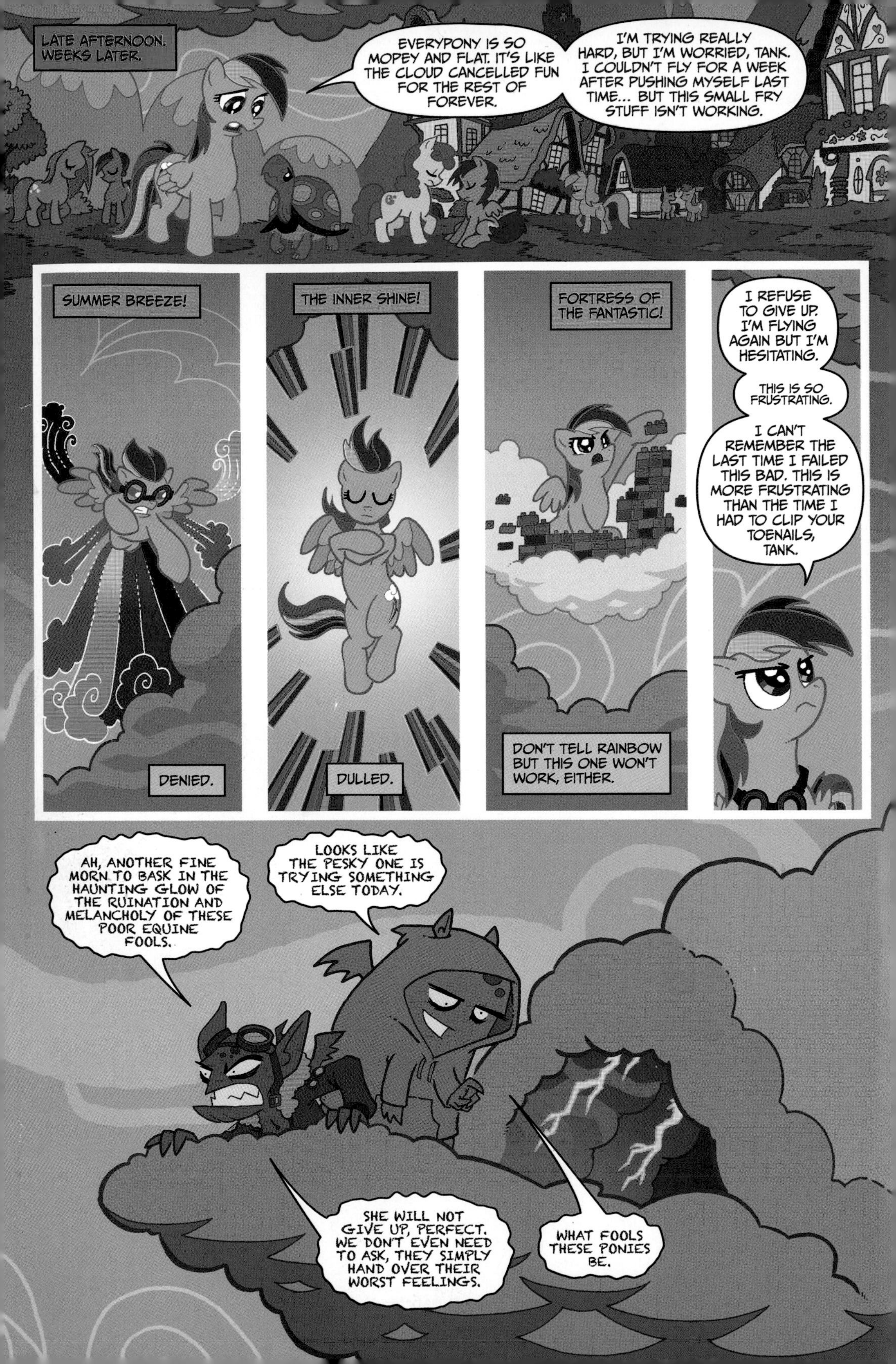
LATE AFTERNOON. WEEKS LATER.
EVERYPONY IS SO MOPEY AND FLAT. IT'S LIKE THE CLOUD CANCELLED FUN FOR THE REST OF FOREVER.
I'M TRYING REALLY HARD, BUT I'M WORRIED, TANK. I COULDN'T FLY FOR A WEEK AFTER PUSHING MYSELF LAST TIME... BUT THIS SMALL FRY STUFF ISN'T WORKING.
SUMMER BREEZE!
DENIED.
THE INNER SHINE!
DULLED.
FORTRESS OF THE FANTASTIC!
DON'T TELL RAINBOW BUT THIS ONE WON'T WORK, EITHER.
I REFUSE TO GIVE UP. I'M FLYING AGAIN BUT I'M HESITATING.
THIS IS SO FRUSTRATING.
I CAN'T REMEMBER THE LAST TIME I FAILED THIS BAD. THIS IS MORE FRUSTRATING THAN THE TIME I HAD TO CLIP YOUR TOENAILS, TANK.
AH, ANOTHER FINE MORN TO BASK IN THE HAUNTING GLOW OF THE RUINATION AND MELANCHOLY OF THESE POOR EQUINE FOOLS.
LOOKS LIKE THE PESKY ONE IS TRYING SOMETHING ELSE TODAY.
SHE WILL NOT GIVE UP, PERFECT. WE DON'T EVEN NEED TO ASK, THEY SIMPLY HAND OVER THEIR WORST FEELINGS.
WHAT FOOLS THESE PONIES BE.

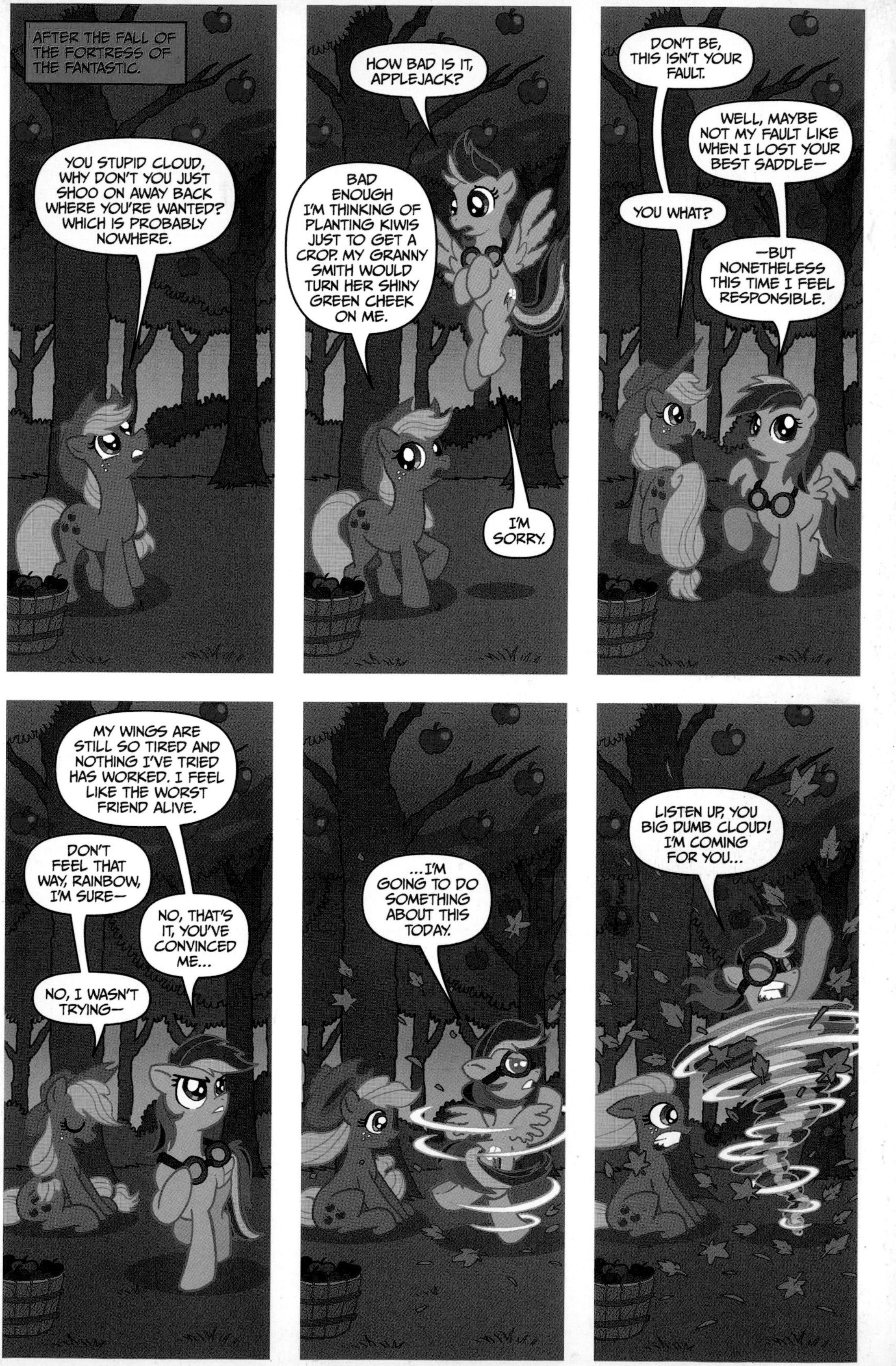
AFTER THE FALL OF THE FORTRESS OF THE FANTASTIC.
YOU STUPID CLOUD, WHY DON'T YOU JUST SHOO ON AWAY BACK WHERE YOU'RE WANTED? WHICH IS PROBABLY NOWHERE.
HOW BAD IS IT, APPLEJACK?
BAD ENOUGH I'M THINKING OF PLANTING KIWIS JUST TO GET A CROP. MY GRANNY SMITH WOULD TURN HER SHINY GREEN CHEEK ON ME.
I'M SORRY.
DON'T BE, THIS ISN'T YOUR FAULT.
WELL, MAYBE NOT MY FAULT LIKE WHEN I LOST YOUR BEST SADDLE—
YOU WHAT?
—BUT NONETHELESS THIS TIME I FEEL RESPONSIBLE.
MY WINGS ARE STILL SO TIRED AND NOTHING I'VE TRIED HAS WORKED. I FEEL LIKE THE WORST FRIEND ALIVE.
DON'T FEEL THAT WAY, RAINBOW, I'M SURE—
NO, THAT'S IT, YOU'VE CONVINCED ME...
NO, I WASN'T TRYING—
...I'M GOING TO DO SOMETHING ABOUT THIS TODAY.
LISTEN UP, YOU BIG DUMB CLOUD! I'M COMING FOR YOU...

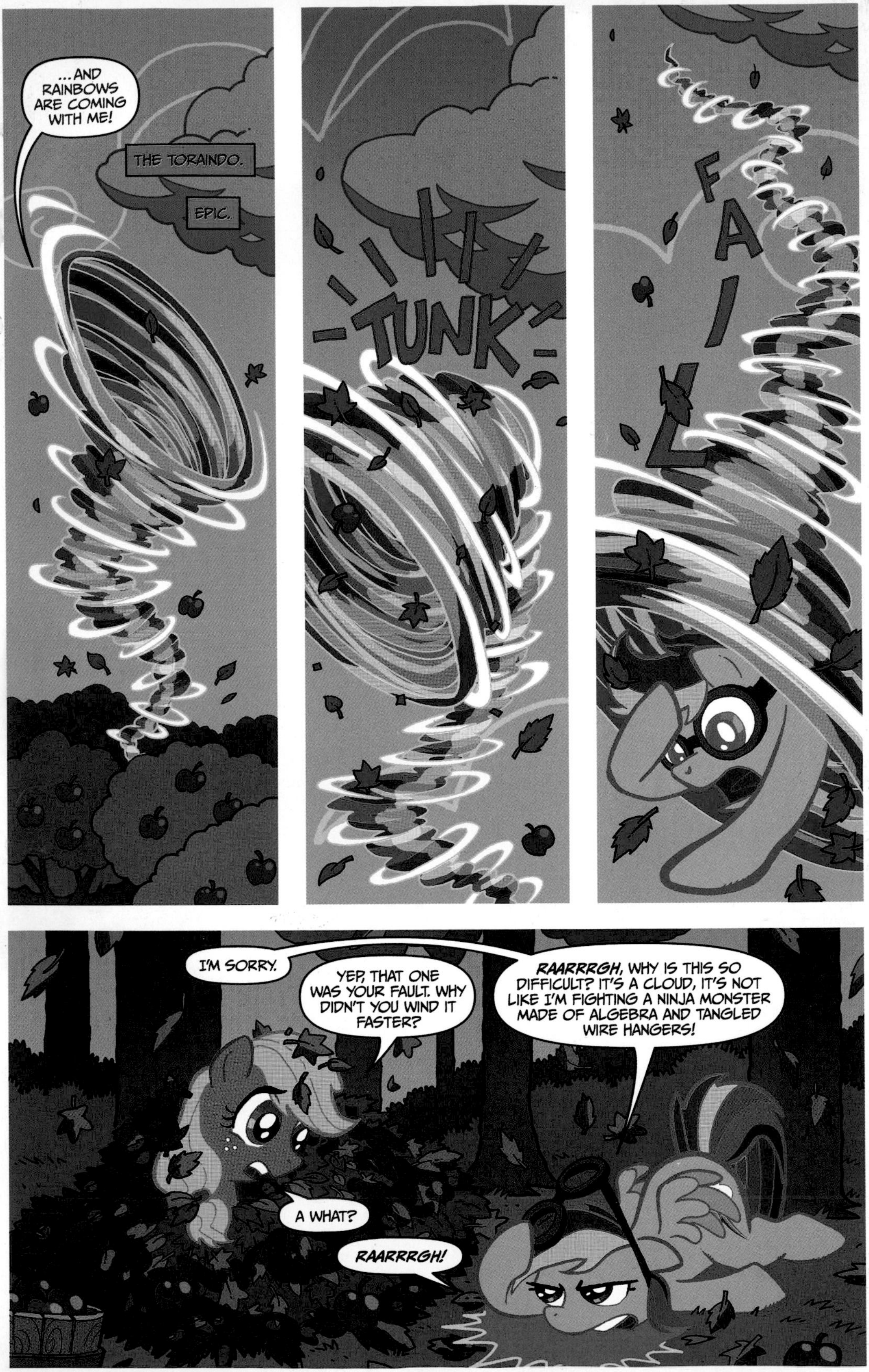
...AND RAINBOWS ARE COMING WITH ME!
THE TORAINDO.
EPIC.
TUNK
FAIL
I'M SORRY.
YEP, THAT ONE WAS YOUR FAULT. WHY DIDN'T YOU WIND IT FASTER?
RAARRRGH, WHY IS THIS SO DIFFICULT? IT'S A CLOUD, IT'S NOT LIKE I'M FIGHTING A NINJA MONSTER MADE OF ALGEBRA AND TANGLED WIRE HANGERS!
A WHAT?
RAARRRGH!

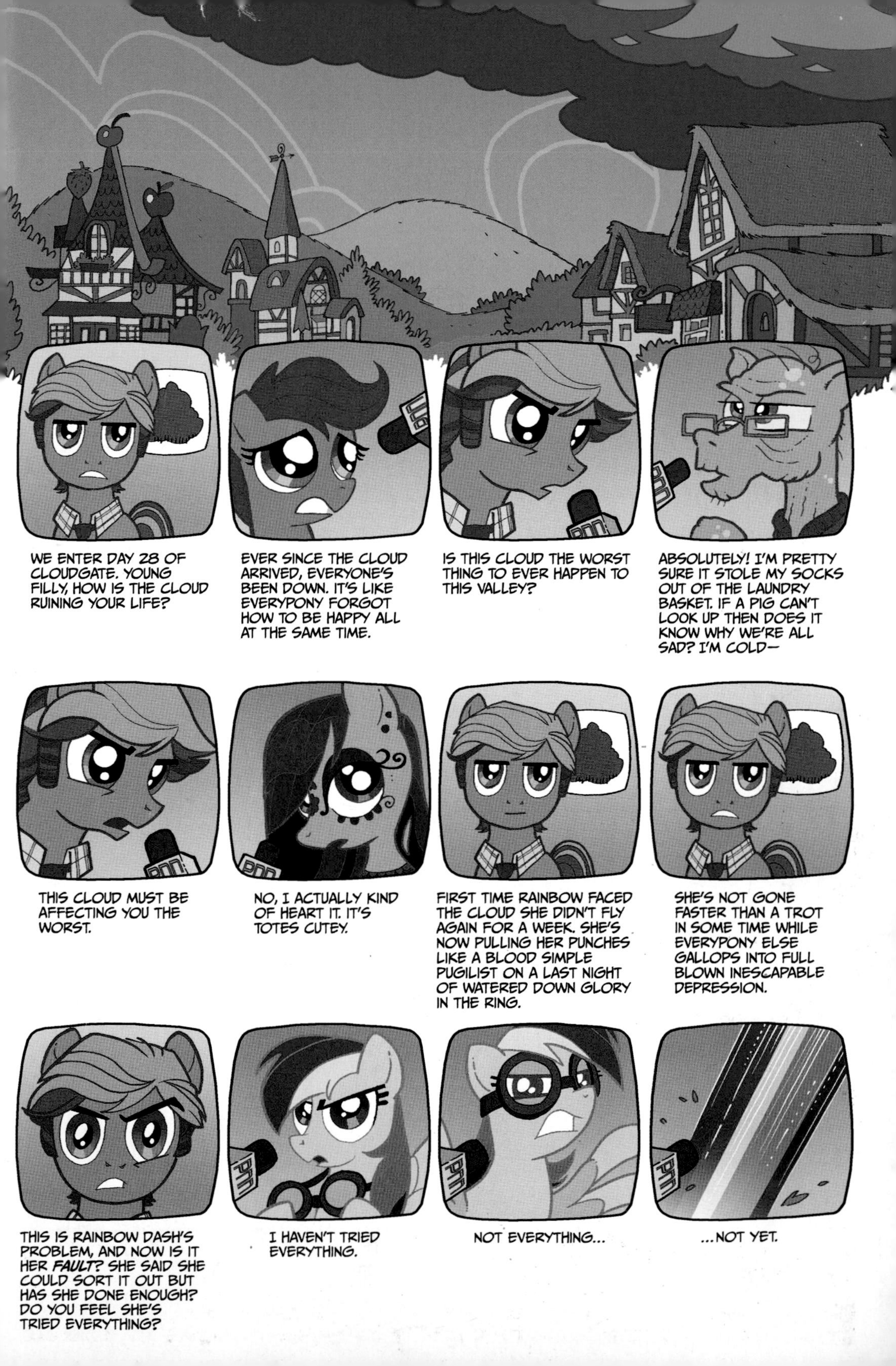

WE ENTER DAY 28 OF CLOUDGATE. YOUNG FILLY, HOW IS THE CLOUD RUINING YOUR LIFE?
EVER SINCE THE CLOUD ARRIVED, EVERYONE'S BEEN DOWN. IT'S LIKE EVERYPONY FORGOT HOW TO BE HAPPY ALL AT THE SAME TIME.
IS THIS CLOUD THE WORST THING TO EVER HAPPEN TO THIS VALLEY?
ABSOLUTELY! I'M PRETTY SURE IT STOLE MY SOCKS OUT OF THE LAUNDRY BASKET. IF A PIG CAN'T LOOK UP THEN DOES IT KNOW WHY WE'RE ALL SAD? I'M COLD—
THIS CLOUD MUST BE AFFECTING YOU THE WORST.
NO, I ACTUALLY KIND OF HEART IT. IT'S TOTES CUTEY.
FIRST TIME RAINBOW FACED THE CLOUD SHE DIDN'T FLY AGAIN FOR A WEEK. SHE'S NOW PULLING HER PUNCHES LIKE A BLOOD SIMPLE PUGILIST ON A LAST NIGHT OF WATERED DOWN GLORY IN THE RING.
SHE'S NOT GONE FASTER THAN A TROT IN SOME TIME WHILE EVERYPONY ELSE GALLOPS INTO FULL BLOWN INESCAPABLE DEPRESSION.
THIS IS RAINBOW DASH'S PROBLEM, AND NOW IS IT HER *FAULT*? SHE SAID SHE COULD SORT IT OUT BUT HAS SHE DONE ENOUGH? DO YOU FEEL SHE'S TRIED EVERYTHING?
I HAVEN'T TRIED EVERYTHING.
NOT EVERYTHING...
...NOT YET.

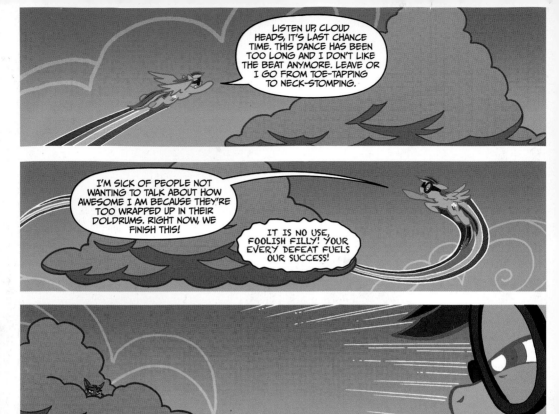

LISTEN UP, CLOUD HEADS, IT'S LAST CHANCE TIME. THIS DANCE HAS BEEN TOO LONG AND I DON'T LIKE THE BEAT ANYMORE. LEAVE OR I GO FROM TOE-TAPPING TO NECK-STOMPING.

I'M SICK OF PEOPLE NOT WANTING TO TALK ABOUT HOW AWESOME I AM BECAUSE THEY'RE TOO WRAPPED UP IN THEIR DOLDRUMS. RIGHT NOW, WE FINISH THIS!

IT IS NO USE, FOOLISH FILLY! YOUR EVERY DEFEAT FUELS OUR SUCCESS!

IT'S LIKE MULE TZU SAYS IN 'THE START OF WAR'...

FACE

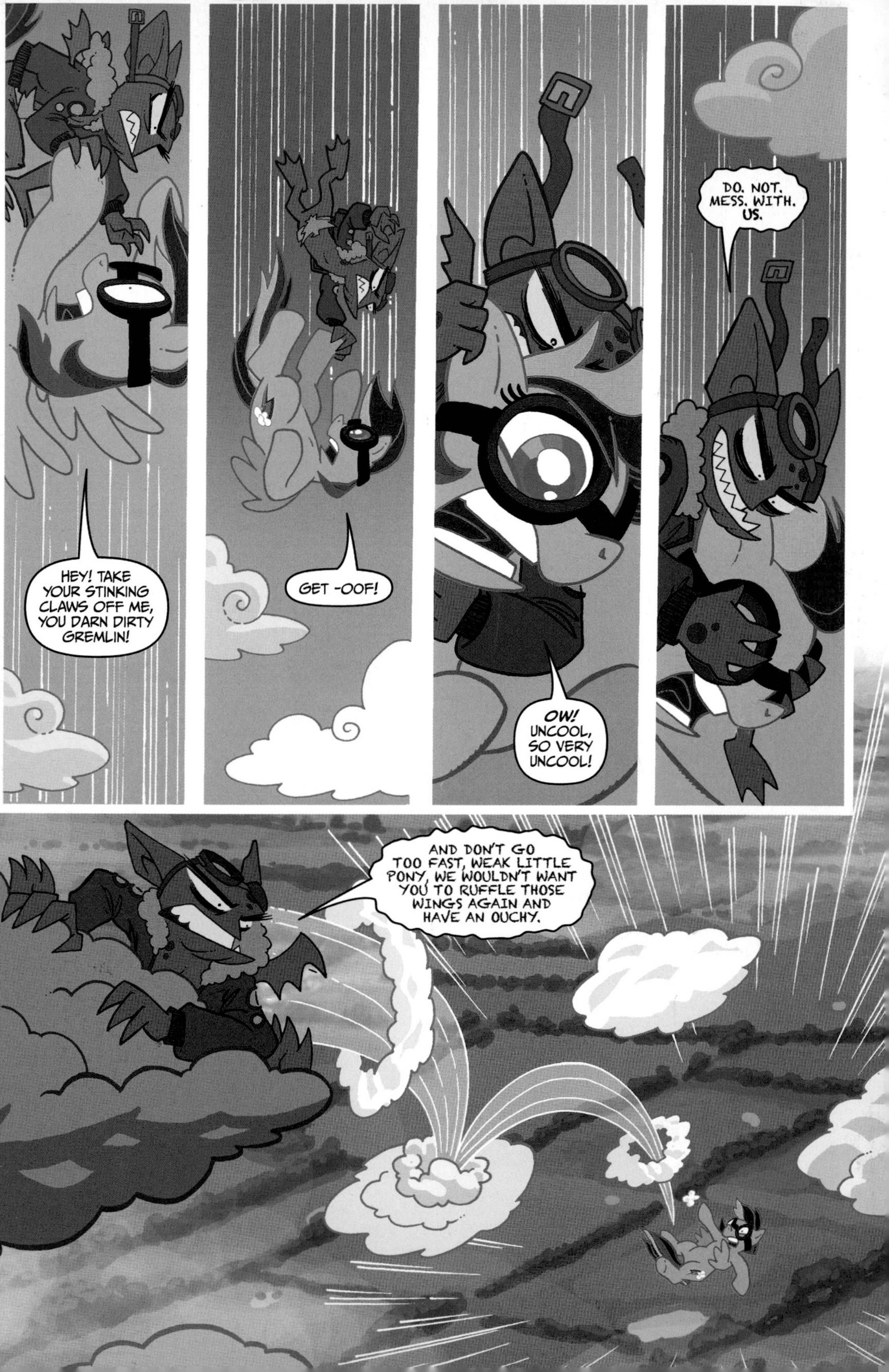
HEY! TAKE YOUR STINKING CLAWS OFF ME, YOU DARN DIRTY GREMLIN!
GET -OOF!
OW! UNCOOL, SO VERY UNCOOL!
DO. NOT. MESS. WITH. US.
AND DON'T GO TOO FAST, WEAK LITTLE PONY, WE WOULDN'T WANT YOU TO RUFFLE THOSE WINGS AGAIN AND HAVE AN OUCHY.

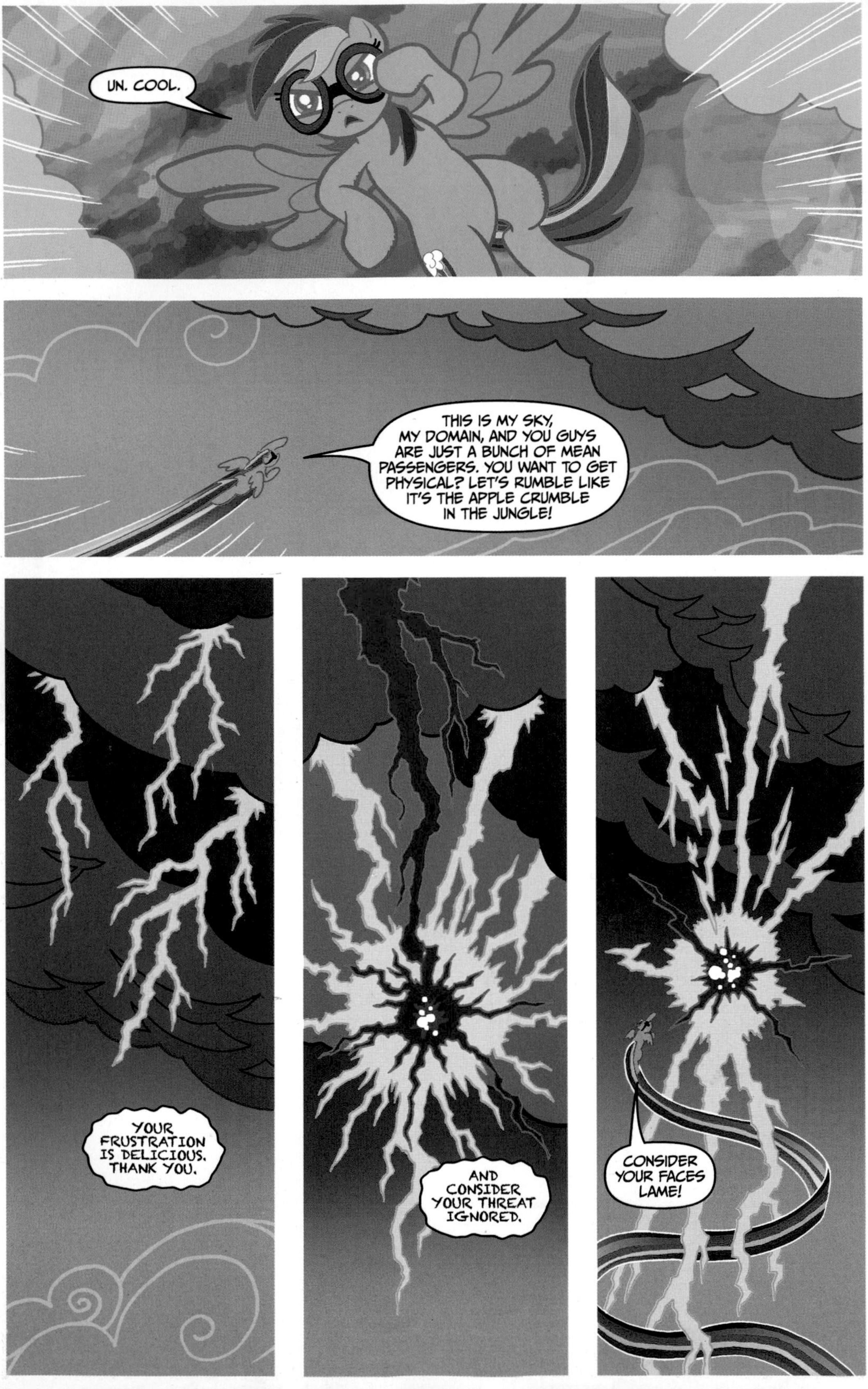
UN. COOL.
THIS IS MY SKY, MY DOMAIN, AND YOU GUYS ARE JUST A BUNCH OF MEAN PASSENGERS. YOU WANT TO GET PHYSICAL? LET'S RUMBLE LIKE IT'S THE APPLE CRUMBLE IN THE JUNGLE!
YOUR FRUSTRATION IS DELICIOUS. THANK YOU.
AND CONSIDER YOUR THREAT IGNORED.
CONSIDER YOUR FACES LAME!

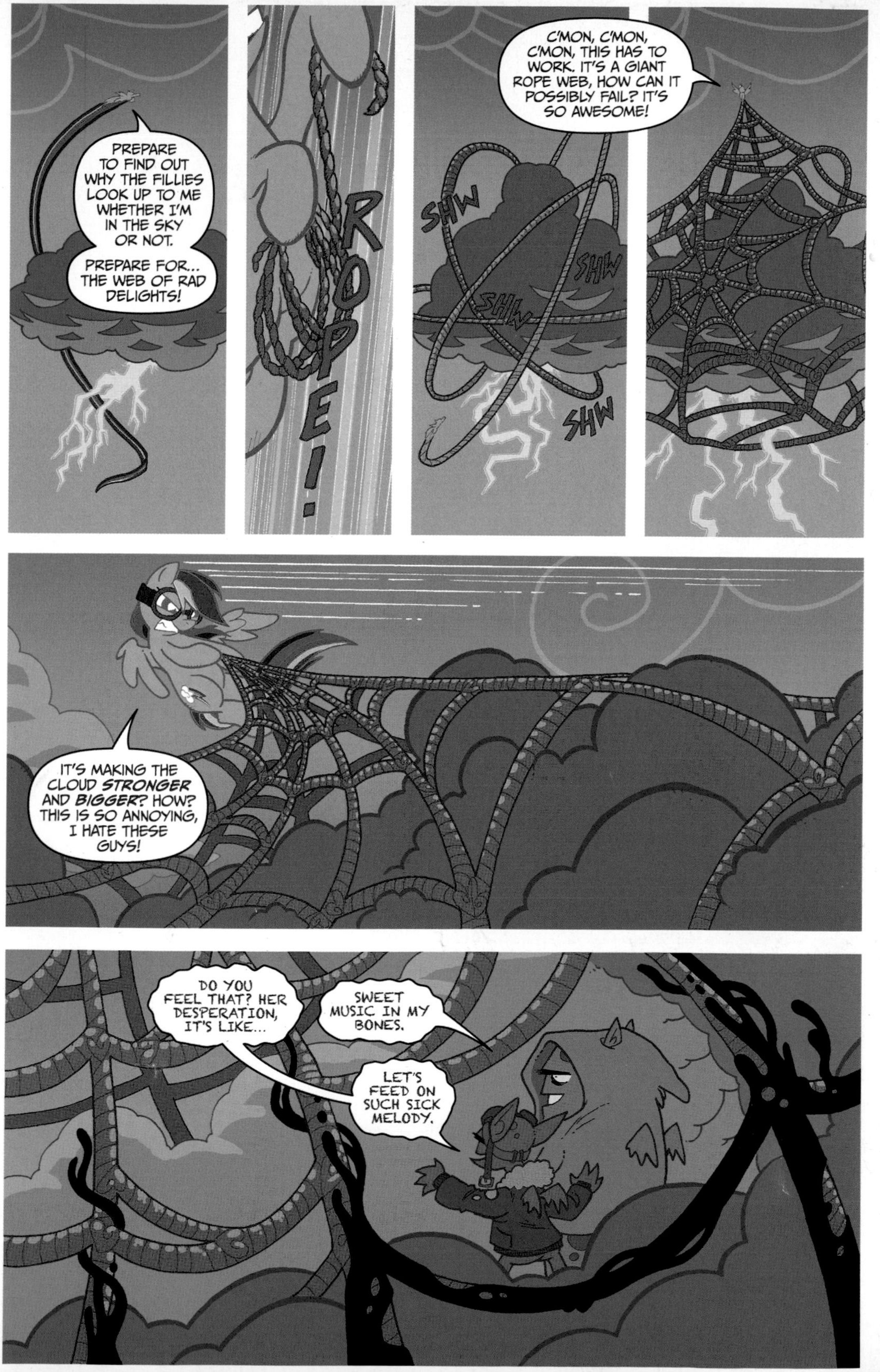
PREPARE TO FIND OUT WHY THE FILLIES LOOK UP TO ME WHETHER I'M IN THE SKY OR NOT.
PREPARE FOR... THE WEB OF RAD DELIGHTS!
ROPE!
C'MON, C'MON, C'MON, THIS HAS TO WORK. IT'S A GIANT ROPE WEB, HOW CAN IT POSSIBLY FAIL? IT'S SO AWESOME!
SHW
SHW
SHW
SHW
IT'S MAKING THE CLOUD STRONGER AND BIGGER? HOW? THIS IS SO ANNOYING, I HATE THESE GUYS!
DO YOU FEEL THAT? HER DESPERATION, IT'S LIKE...
SWEET MUSIC IN MY BONES.
LET'S FEED ON SUCH SICK MELODY.

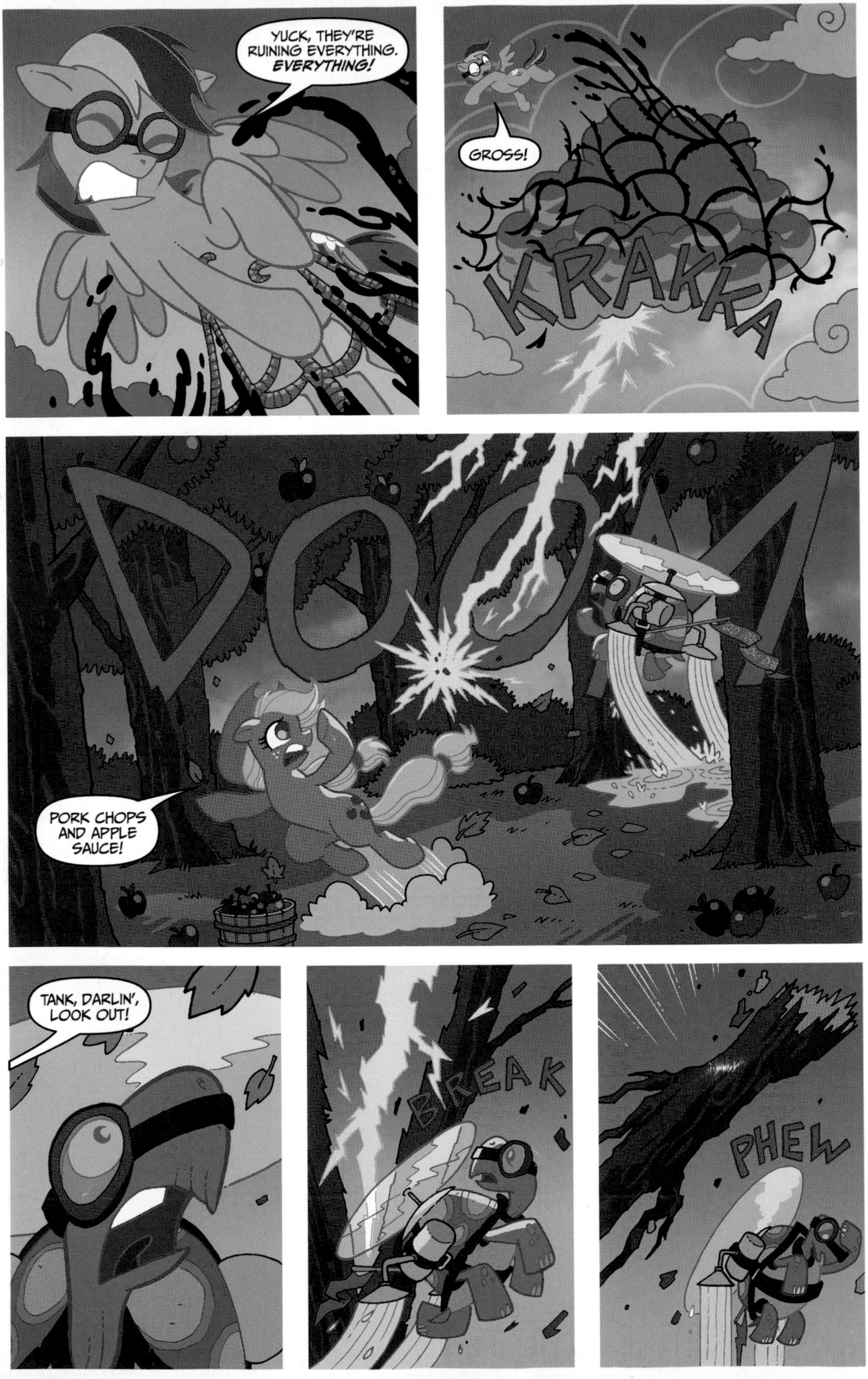
YUCK, THEY'RE RUINING EVERYTHING. *EVERYTHING!*
GROSS!
KRAKKA
DOOM
PORK CHOPS AND APPLE SAUCE!
TANK, DARLIN', LOOK OUT!
BREAK
PHEW

TANK!

TANK, ARE YOU ALRIGHT?

GIVE ME A SIGN.

BROHOOF

I'M SORRY I LET THIS HAPPEN.

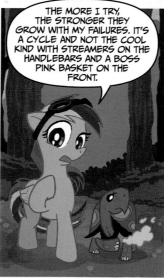

THE MORE I TRY, THE STRONGER THEY GROW WITH MY FAILURES. IT'S A CYCLE AND NOT THE COOL KIND WITH STREAMERS ON THE HANDLEBARS AND A BOSS PINK BASKET ON THE FRONT.

HOW CAN I BEAT THESE GREMLINS IF EVERY ATTEMPT MAKES THEM STRONGER? OUR NEGATIVITY POWERS THEM SO SURELY SOME POSITIVITY WOULD BREAK THEM.

BUT WHERE ARE WE GOING TO FIND POSITIVE THOUGHTS NOW?

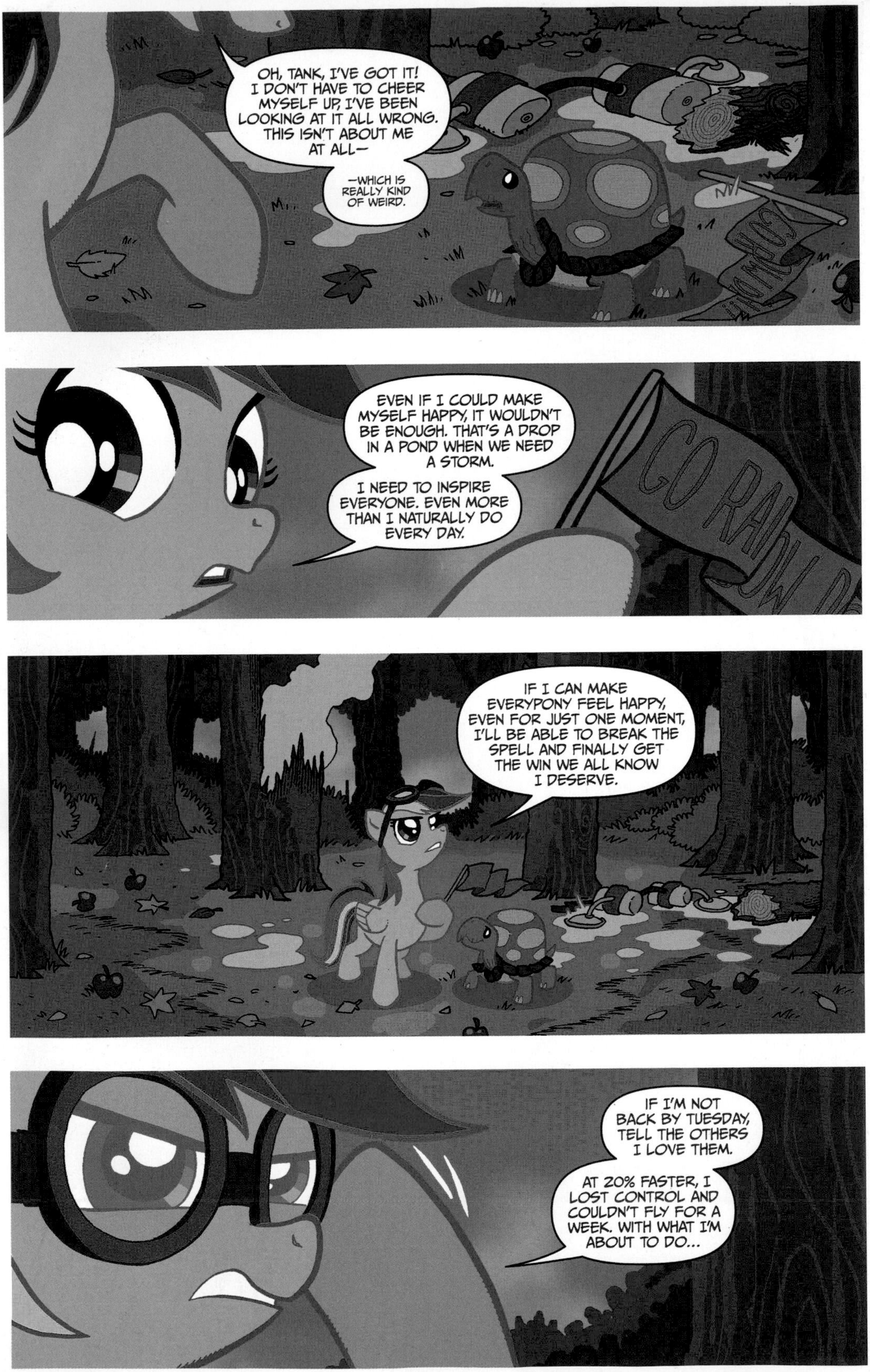
OH, TANK, I'VE GOT IT! I DON'T HAVE TO CHEER MYSELF UP, I'VE BEEN LOOKING AT IT ALL WRONG. THIS ISN'T ABOUT ME AT ALL—
—WHICH IS REALLY KIND OF WEIRD.
EVEN IF I COULD MAKE MYSELF HAPPY, IT WOULDN'T BE ENOUGH. THAT'S A DROP IN A POND WHEN WE NEED A STORM.
I NEED TO INSPIRE EVERYONE. EVEN MORE THAN I NATURALLY DO EVERY DAY.
IF I CAN MAKE EVERYPONY FEEL HAPPY, EVEN FOR JUST ONE MOMENT, I'LL BE ABLE TO BREAK THE SPELL AND FINALLY GET THE WIN WE ALL KNOW I DESERVE.
IF I'M NOT BACK BY TUESDAY, TELL THE OTHERS I LOVE THEM.
AT 20% FASTER, I LOST CONTROL AND COULDN'T FLY FOR A WEEK. WITH WHAT I'M ABOUT TO DO...

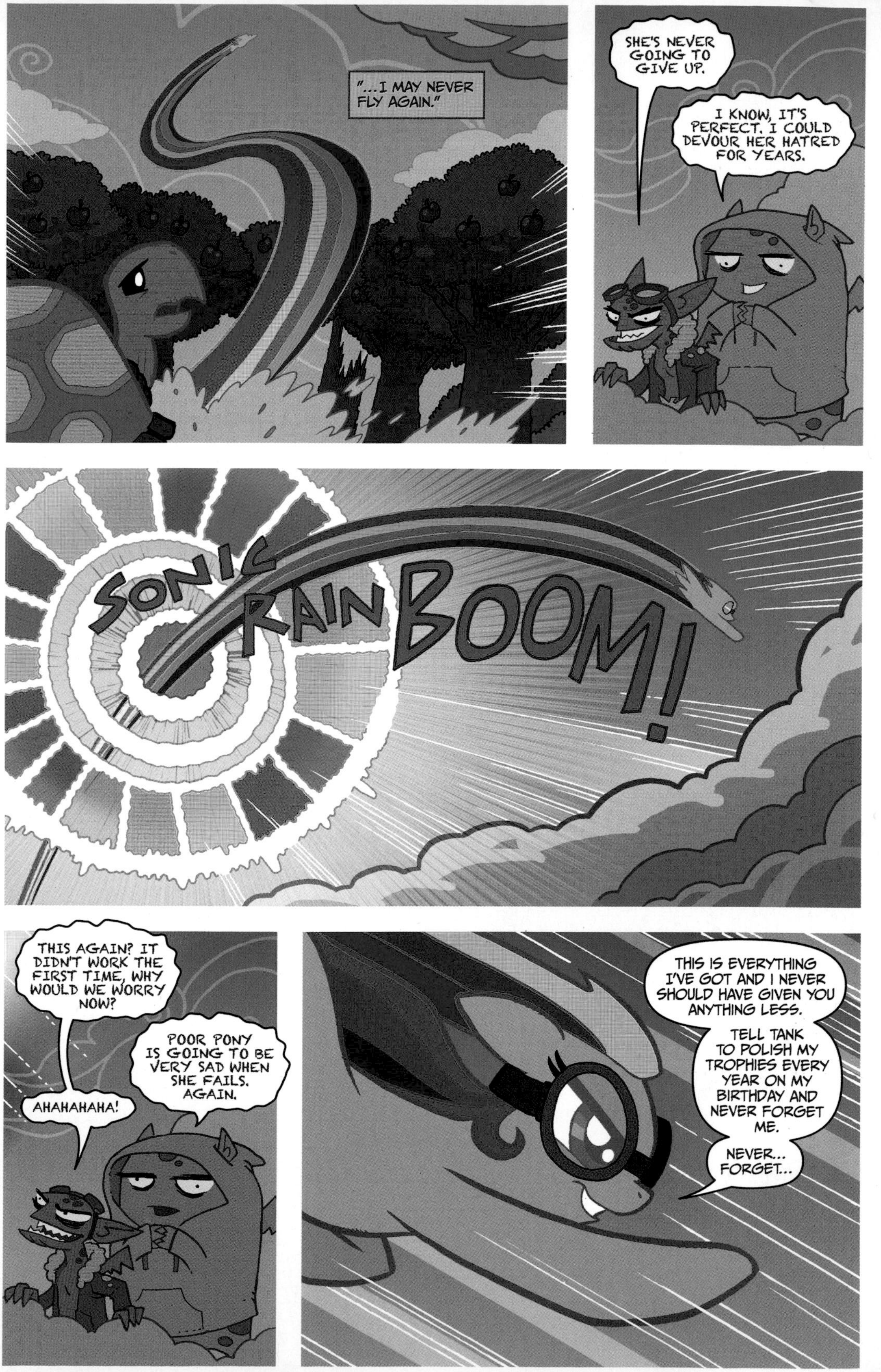
"...I MAY NEVER FLY AGAIN."
SHE'S NEVER GOING TO GIVE UP.
I KNOW, IT'S PERFECT. I COULD DEVOUR HER HATRED FOR YEARS.
SONIC RAINBOOM!
THIS AGAIN? IT DIDN'T WORK THE FIRST TIME, WHY WOULD WE WORRY NOW?
POOR PONY IS GOING TO BE VERY SAD WHEN SHE FAILS. AGAIN.
AHAHAHAHA!
THIS IS EVERYTHING I'VE GOT AND I NEVER SHOULD HAVE GIVEN YOU ANYTHING LESS.
TELL TANK TO POLISH MY TROPHIES EVERY YEAR ON MY BIRTHDAY AND NEVER FORGET ME.
NEVER... FORGET...

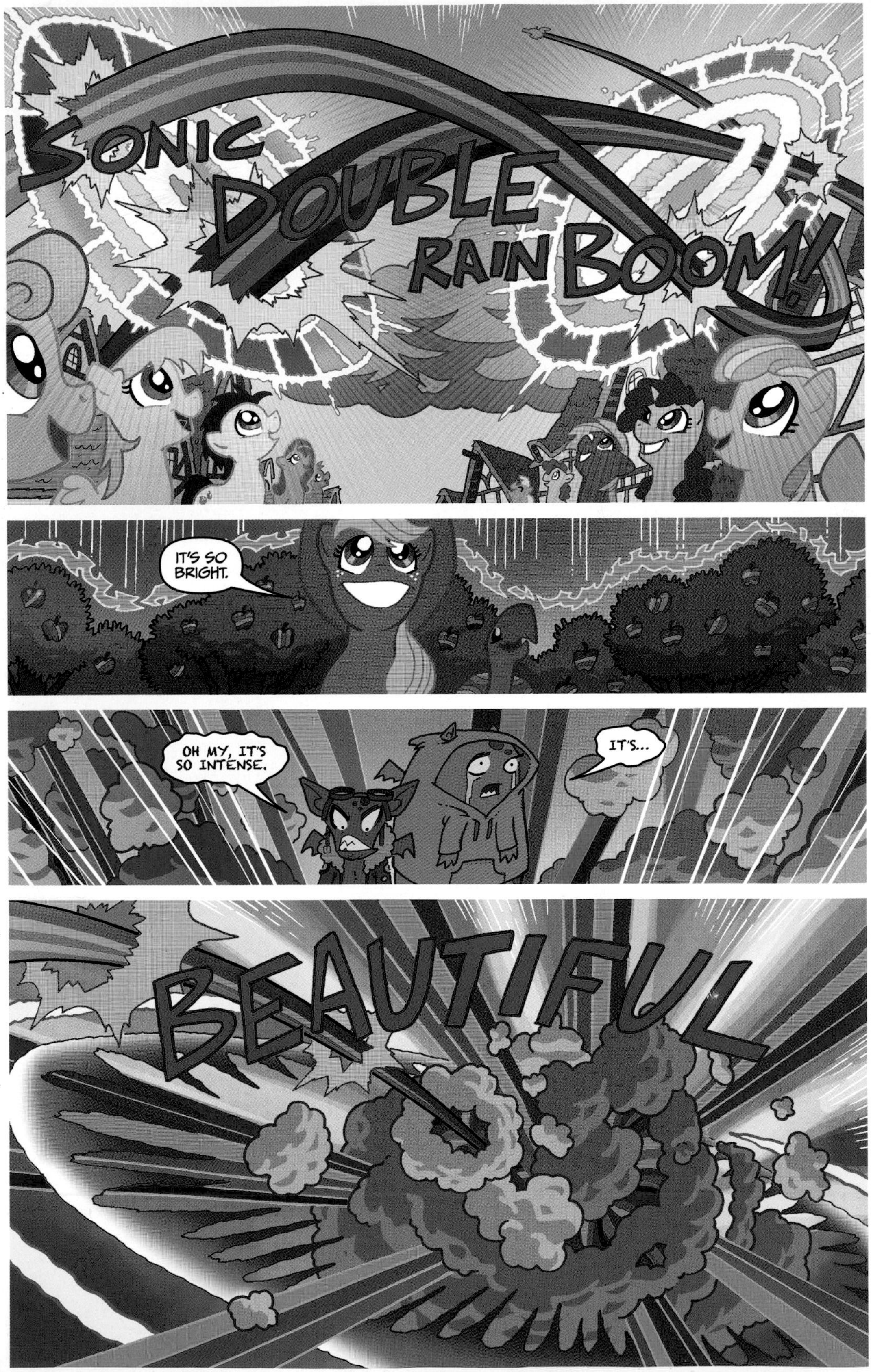
SONIC DOUBLE RAINBOOM!
IT'S SO BRIGHT.
OH MY, IT'S SO INTENSE.
IT'S...
BEAUTIFUL

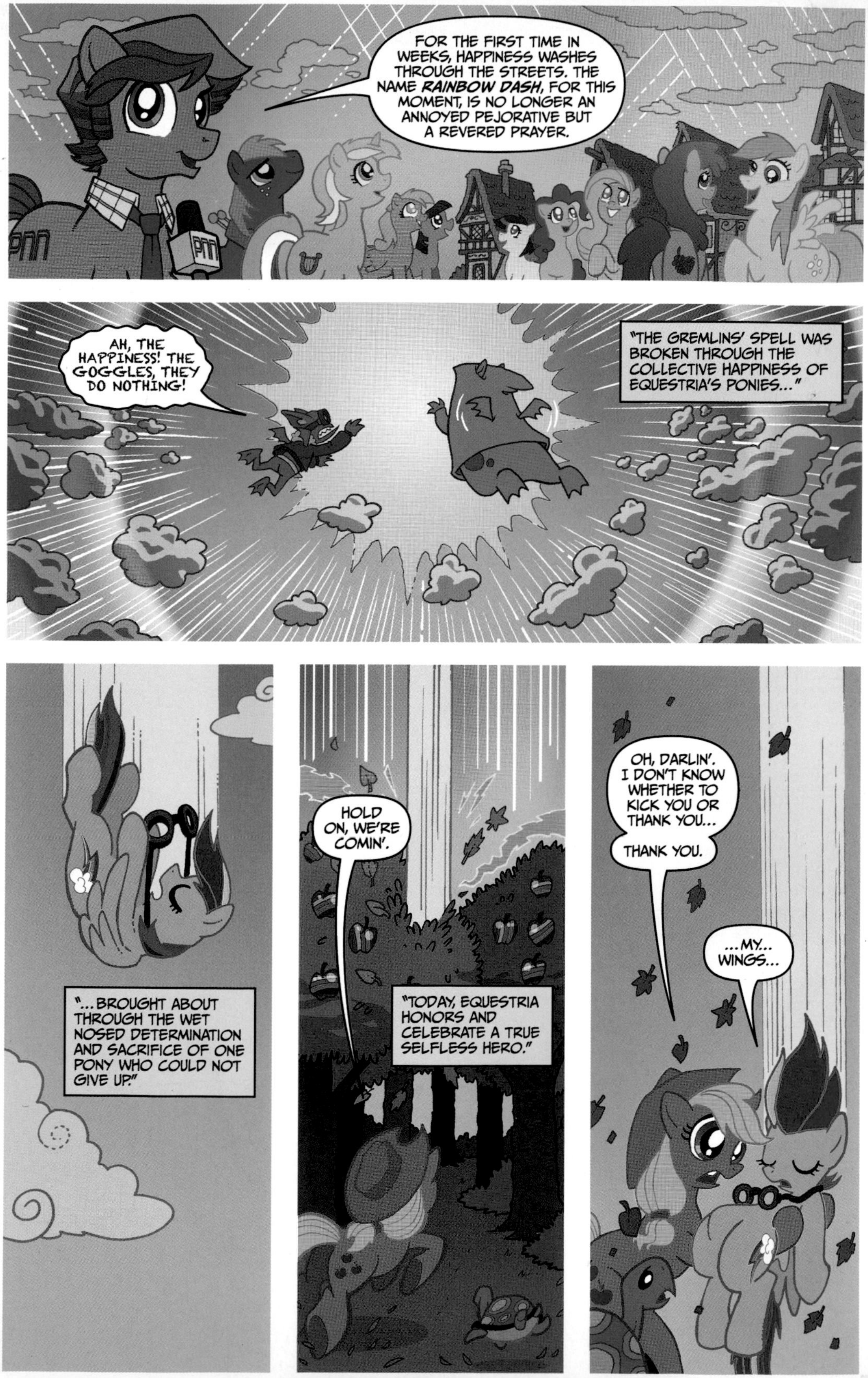
FOR THE FIRST TIME IN WEEKS, HAPPINESS WASHES THROUGH THE STREETS. THE NAME RAINBOW DASH, FOR THIS MOMENT, IS NO LONGER AN ANNOYED PEJORATIVE BUT A REVERED PRAYER.
PNN
AH, THE HAPPINESS! THE GOGGLES, THEY DO NOTHING!
"THE GREMLINS' SPELL WAS BROKEN THROUGH THE COLLECTIVE HAPPINESS OF EQUESTRIA'S PONIES..."
"...BROUGHT ABOUT THROUGH THE WET NOSED DETERMINATION AND SACRIFICE OF ONE PONY WHO COULD NOT GIVE UP."
HOLD ON, WE'RE COMIN'.
"TODAY, EQUESTRIA HONORS AND CELEBRATE A TRUE SELFLESS HERO."
OH, DARLIN'. I DON'T KNOW WHETHER TO KICK YOU OR THANK YOU...
THANK YOU.
...MY... WINGS...

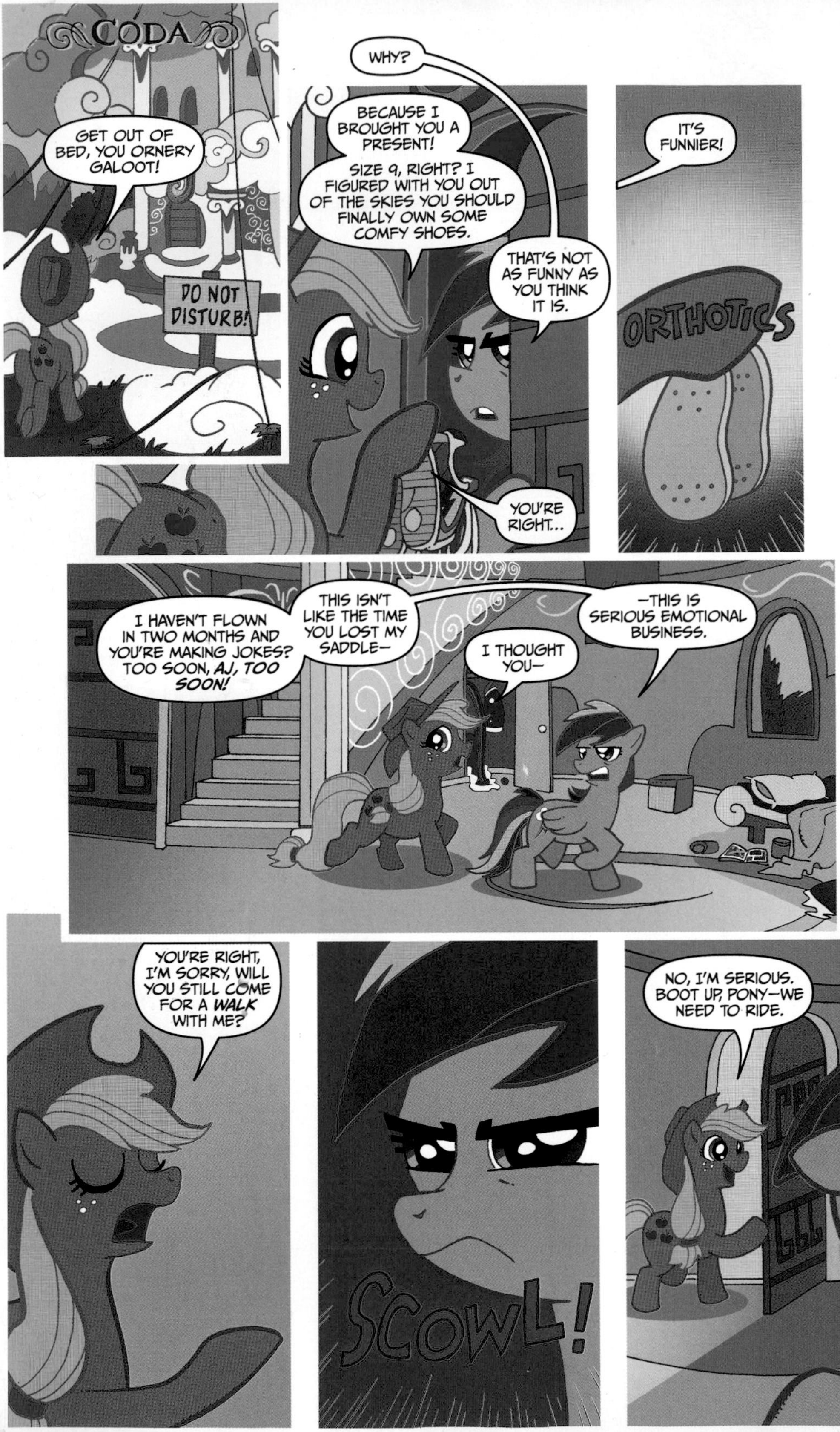
CODA
GET OUT OF BED, YOU ORNERY GALOOT!
DO NOT DISTURB!
WHY?
BECAUSE I BROUGHT YOU A PRESENT!
SIZE 9, RIGHT? I FIGURED WITH YOU OUT OF THE SKIES YOU SHOULD FINALLY OWN SOME COMFY SHOES.
THAT'S NOT AS FUNNY AS YOU THINK IT IS.
YOU'RE RIGHT...
IT'S FUNNIER!
ORTHOTICS
I HAVEN'T FLOWN IN TWO MONTHS AND YOU'RE MAKING JOKES? TOO SOON, AJ, TOO SOON!
THIS ISN'T LIKE THE TIME YOU LOST MY SADDLE—
I THOUGHT YOU—
—THIS IS SERIOUS EMOTIONAL BUSINESS.
YOU'RE RIGHT, I'M SORRY, WILL YOU STILL COME FOR A WALK WITH ME?
SCOWL!
NO, I'M SERIOUS. BOOT UP, PONY—WE NEED TO RIDE.

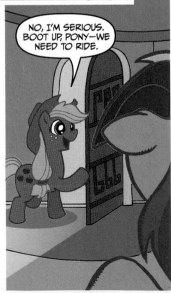

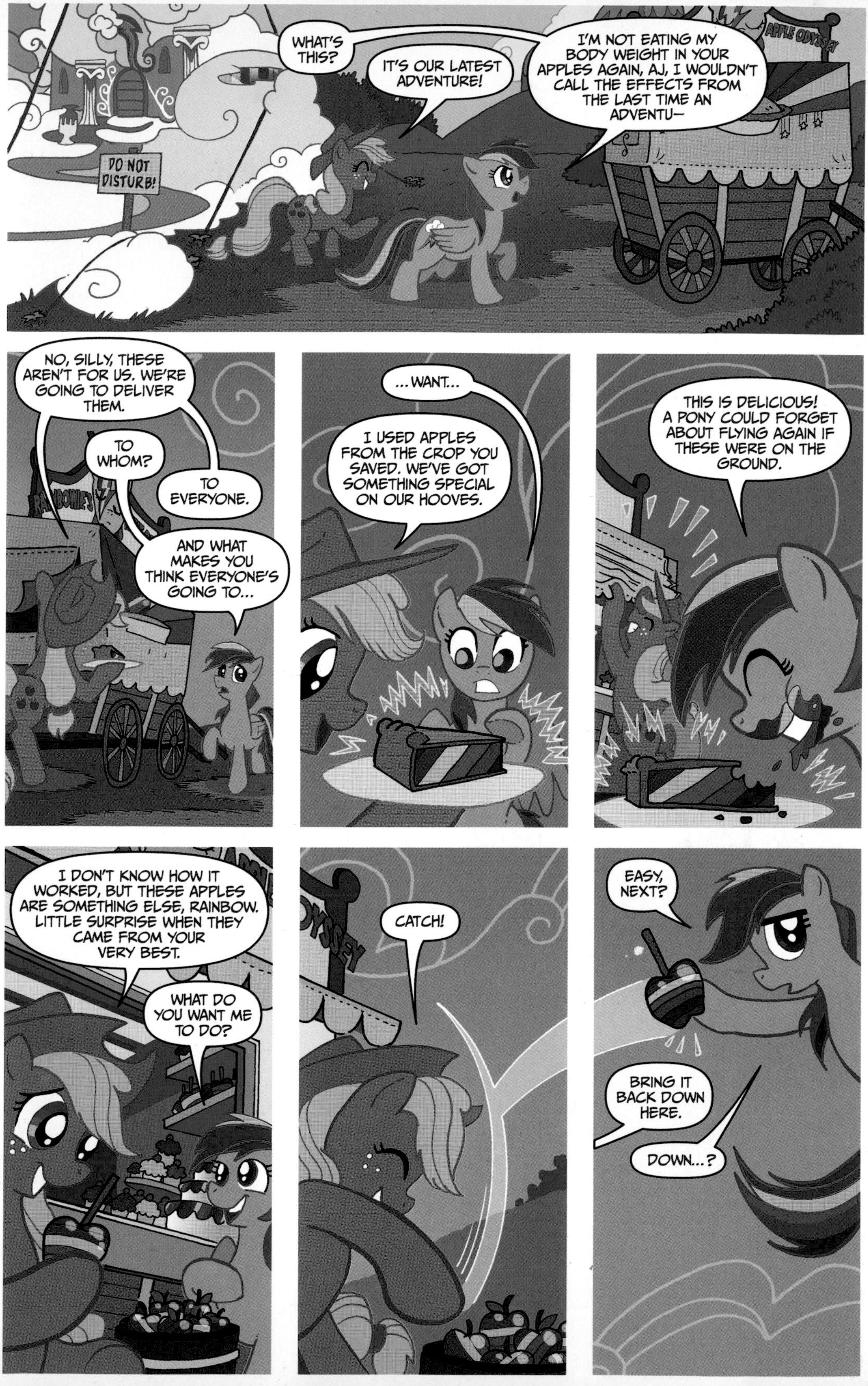
DO NOT DISTURB!
APPLE ODYSSEY
WHAT'S THIS?
IT'S OUR LATEST ADVENTURE!
I'M NOT EATING MY BODY WEIGHT IN YOUR APPLES AGAIN, AJ, I WOULDN'T CALL THE EFFECTS FROM THE LAST TIME AN ADVENTU–
NO, SILLY, THESE AREN'T FOR US. WE'RE GOING TO DELIVER THEM.
TO WHOM?
TO EVERYONE.
AND WHAT MAKES YOU THINK EVERYONE'S GOING TO...
...WANT...
I USED APPLES FROM THE CROP YOU SAVED. WE'VE GOT SOMETHING SPECIAL ON OUR HOOVES.
THIS IS DELICIOUS! A PONY COULD FORGET ABOUT FLYING AGAIN IF THESE WERE ON THE GROUND.
I DON'T KNOW HOW IT WORKED, BUT THESE APPLES ARE SOMETHING ELSE, RAINBOW. LITTLE SURPRISE WHEN THEY CAME FROM YOUR VERY BEST.
WHAT DO YOU WANT ME TO DO?
CATCH!
EASY, NEXT?
BRING IT BACK DOWN HERE.
DOWN...?

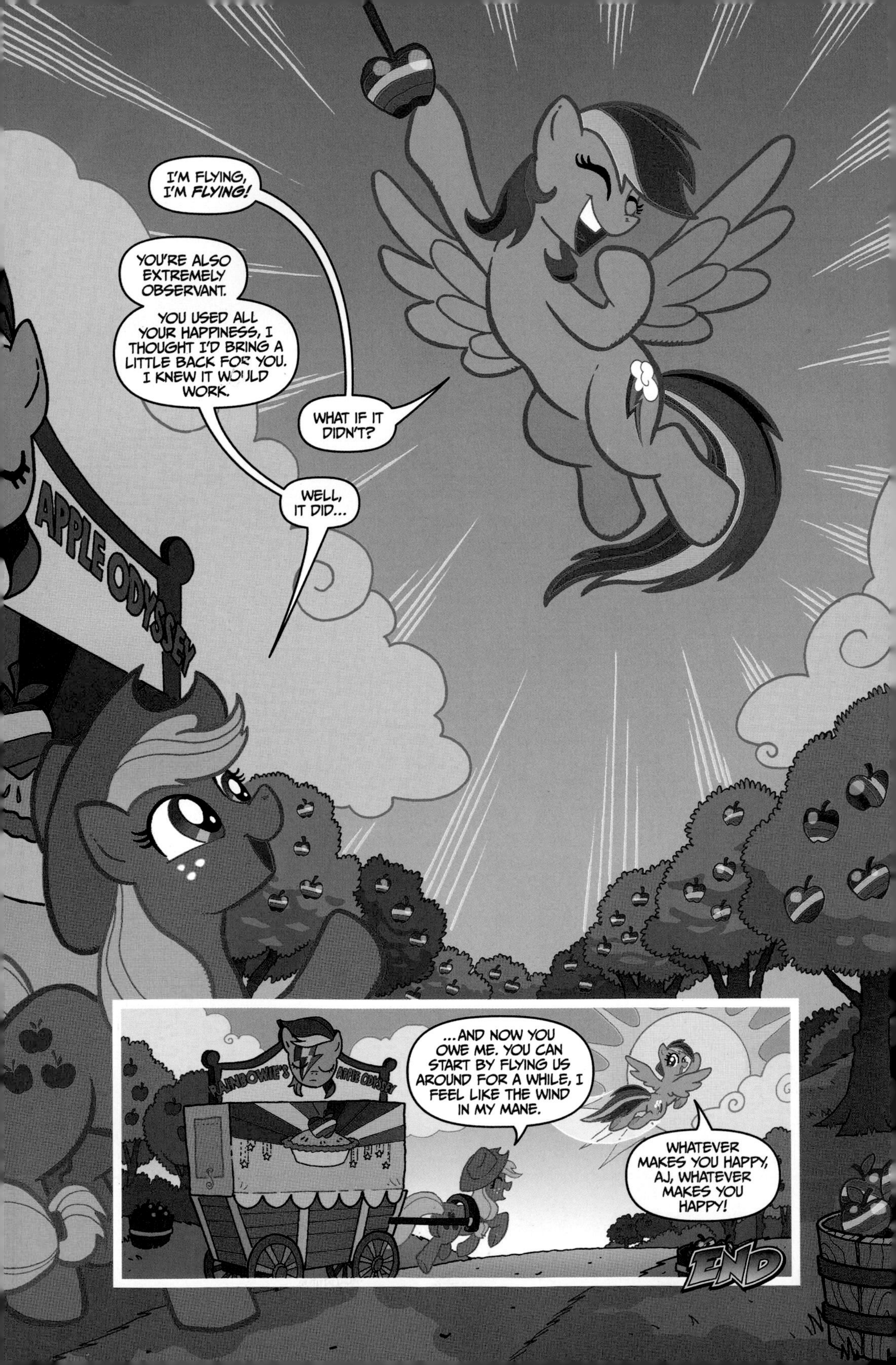

I'M FLYING, I'M FLYING!
YOU'RE ALSO EXTREMELY OBSERVANT.
YOU USED ALL YOUR HAPPINESS, I THOUGHT I'D BRING A LITTLE BACK FOR YOU. I KNEW IT WOULD WORK.
WHAT IF IT DIDN'T?
WELL, IT DID...
APPLE ODYSSEY
RAINBOWIE'S APPLE ODYSSEY
...AND NOW YOU OWE ME. YOU CAN START BY FLYING US AROUND FOR A WHILE, I FEEL LIKE THE WIND IN MY MANE.
WHATEVER MAKES YOU HAPPY, AJ, WHATEVER MAKES YOU HAPPY!
END

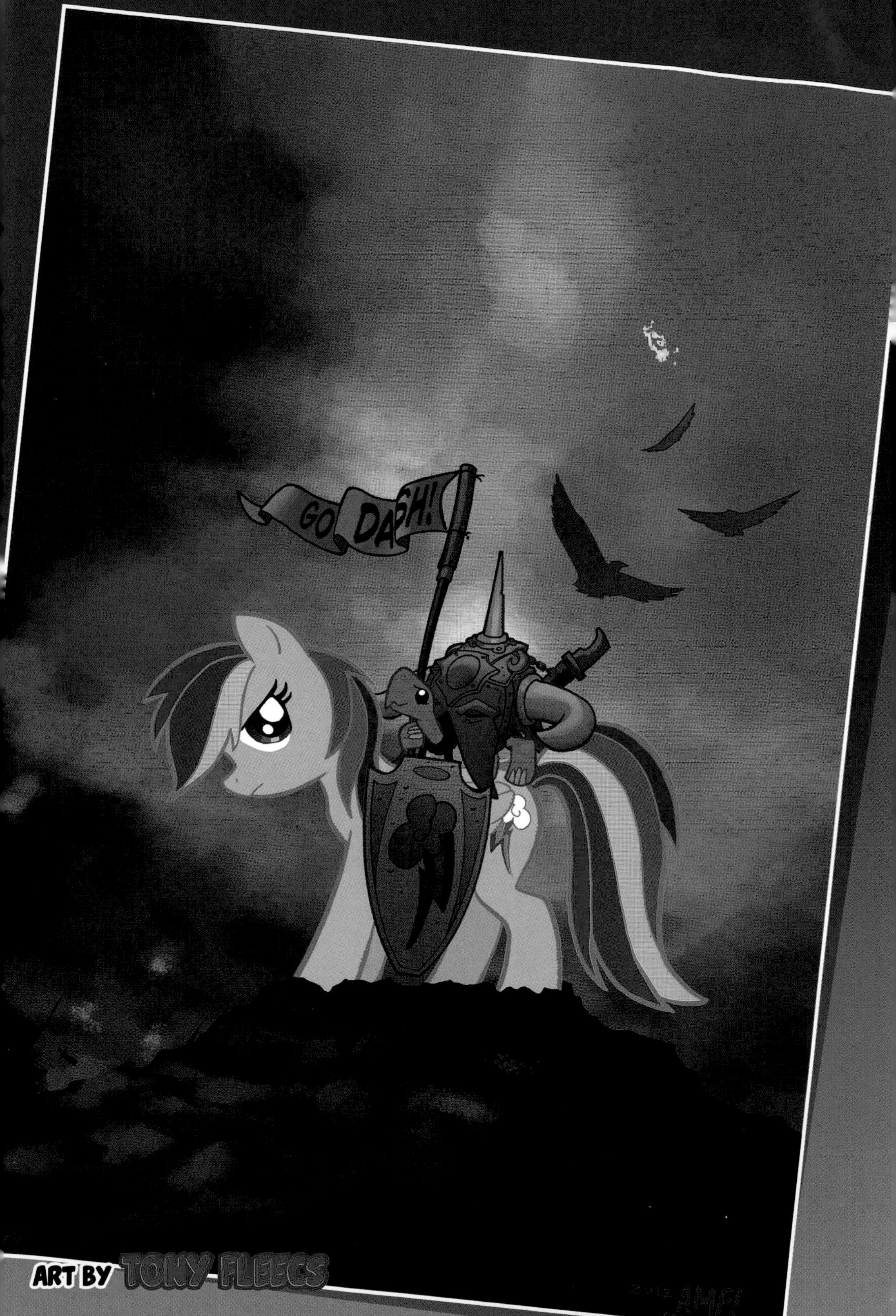
GO DASH!

ART BY TONY FLEECS

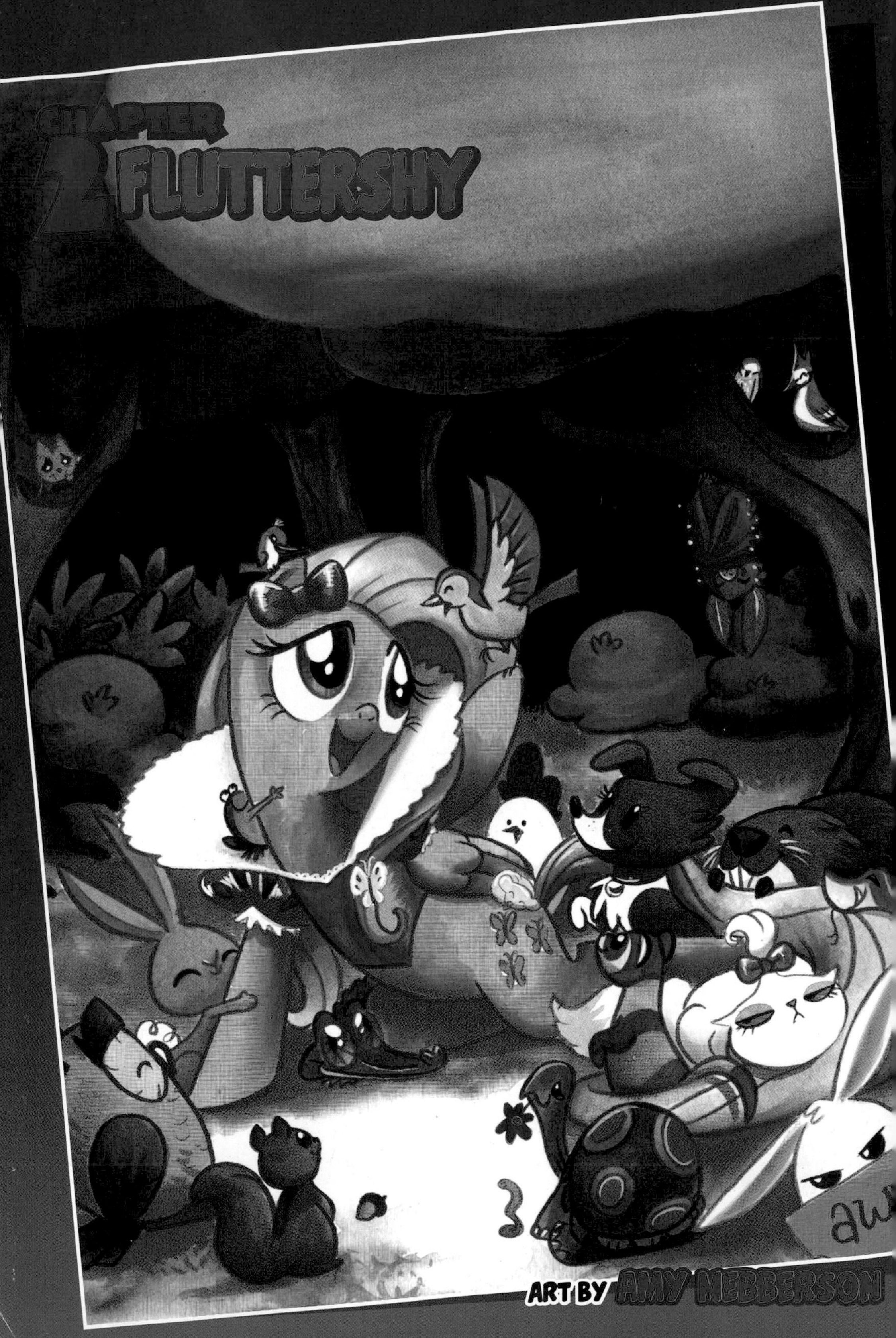
CHAPTER
2 FLUTTERSHY
ART BY AMY MEBBERSON

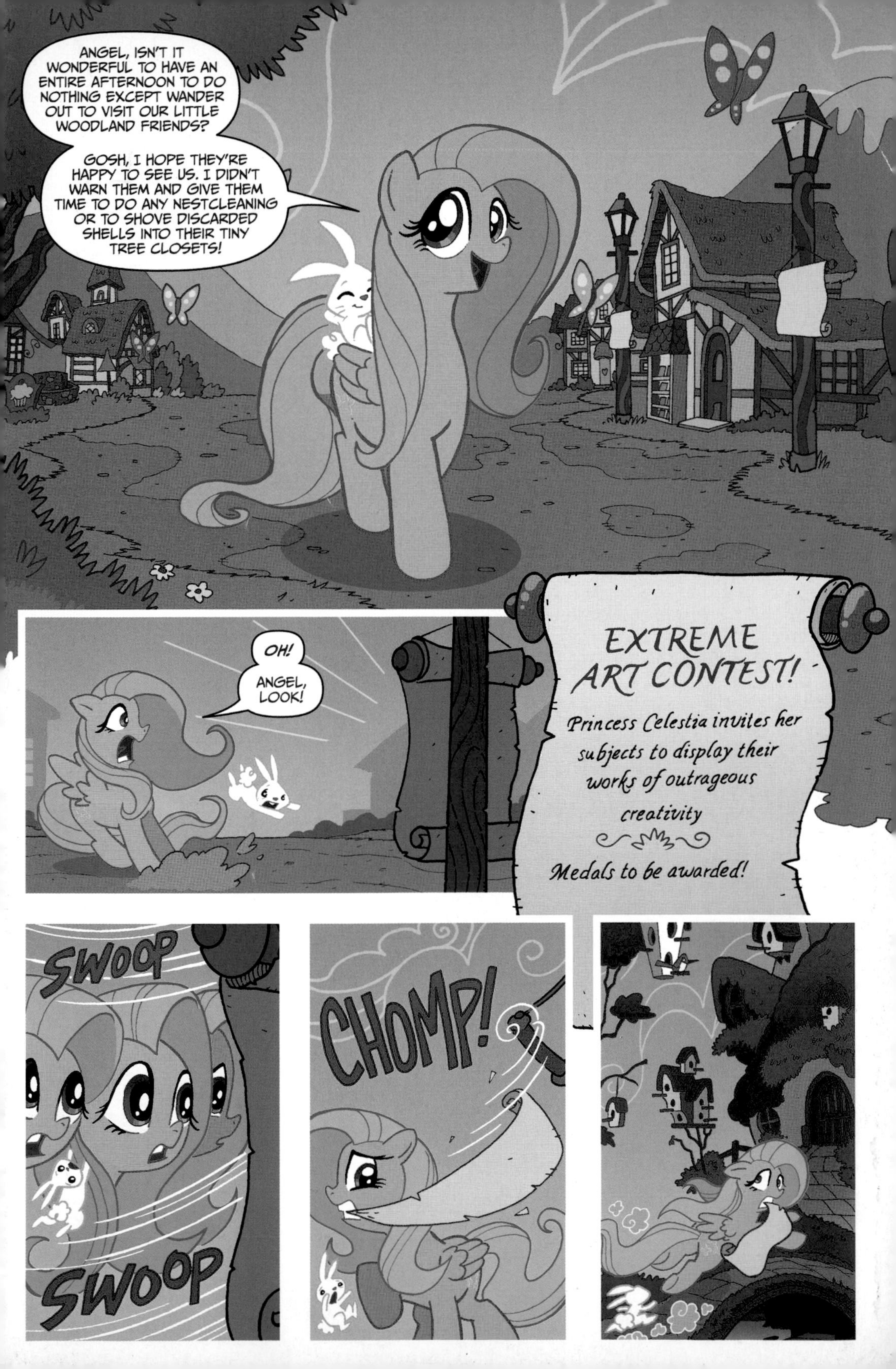
ANGEL, ISN'T IT WONDERFUL TO HAVE AN ENTIRE AFTERNOON TO DO NOTHING EXCEPT WANDER OUT TO VISIT OUR LITTLE WOODLAND FRIENDS?
GOSH, I HOPE THEY'RE HAPPY TO SEE US. I DIDN'T WARN THEM AND GIVE THEM TIME TO DO ANY NESTCLEANING OR TO SHOVE DISCARDED SHELLS INTO THEIR TINY TREE CLOSETS!
OH!
ANGEL, LOOK!
EXTREME ART CONTEST!
Princess Celestia invites her subjects to display their works of outrageous creativity
Medals to be awarded!
SWOOP
SWOOP
CHOMP!

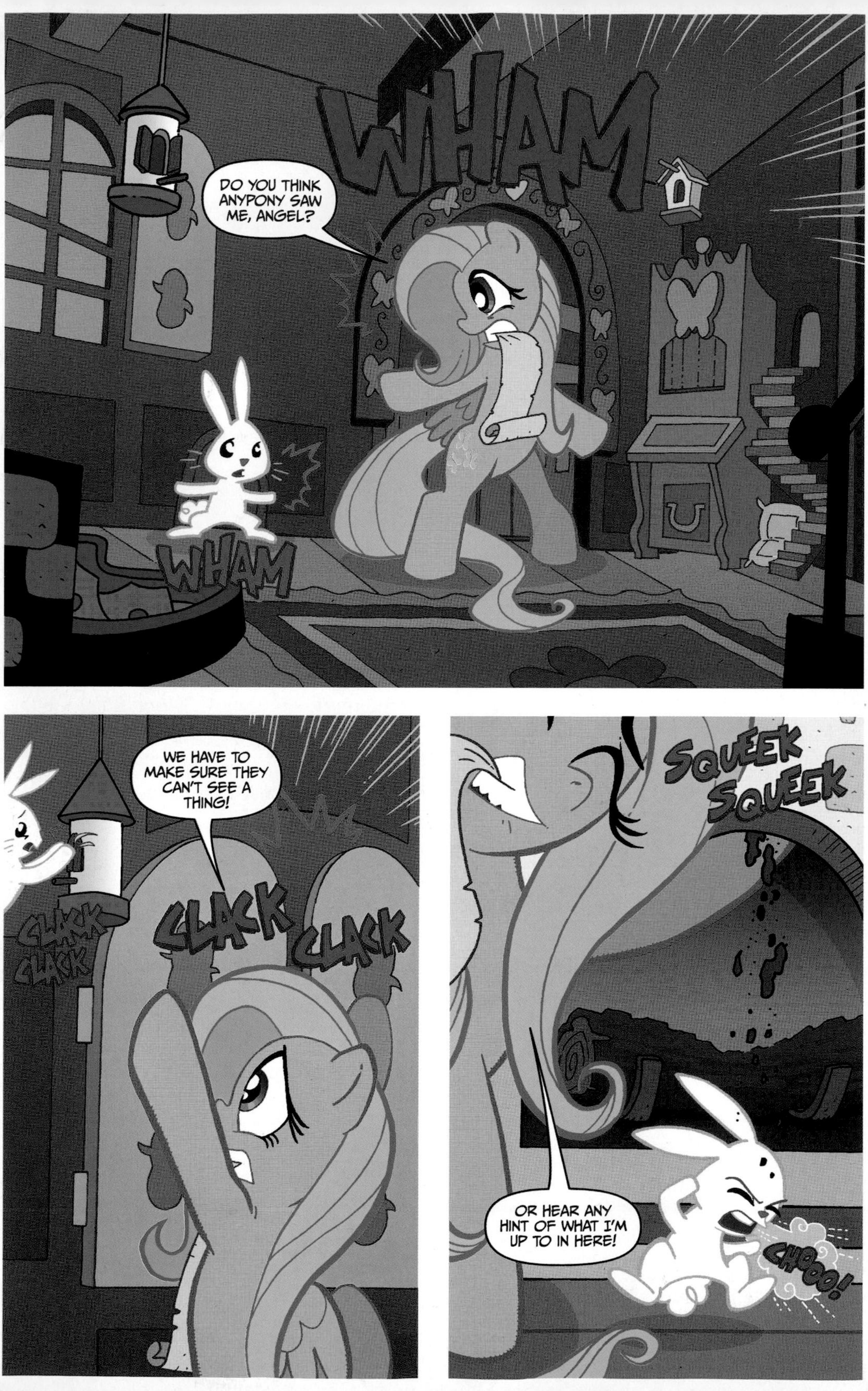
WHAM
DO YOU THINK ANYPONY SAW ME, ANGEL?
WHAM
WE HAVE TO MAKE SURE THEY CAN'T SEE A THING!
CLACK CLACK
CLACK
CLACK
SQUEEK SQUEEK
OR HEAR ANY HINT OF WHAT I'M UP TO IN HERE!
CHOOO!

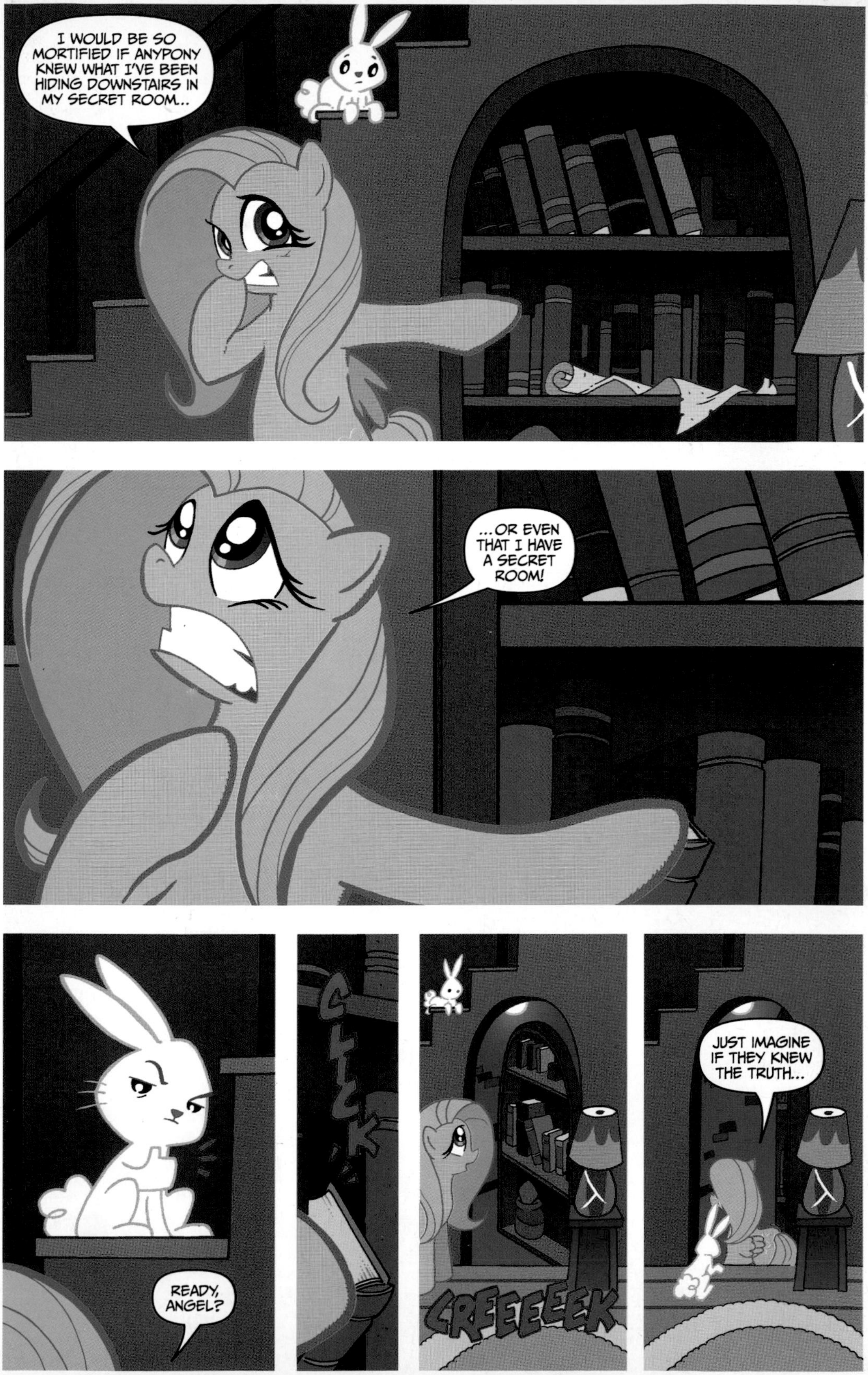
I WOULD BE SO MORTIFIED IF ANYPONY KNEW WHAT I'VE BEEN HIDING DOWNSTAIRS IN MY SECRET ROOM...
...OR EVEN THAT I HAVE A SECRET ROOM!
READY, ANGEL?
CLICK
CREEEEEK
JUST IMAGINE IF THEY KNEW THE TRUTH...

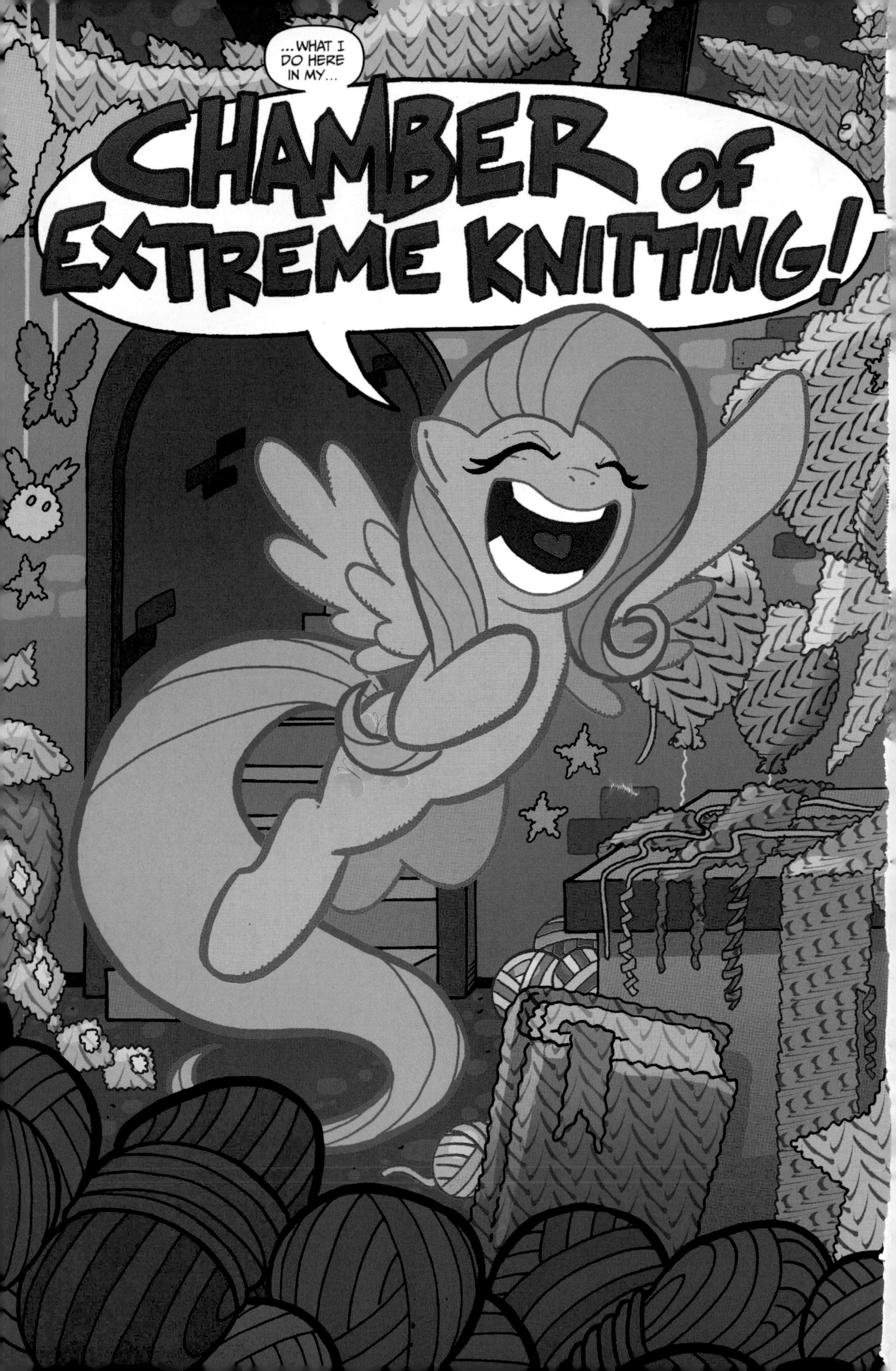
...WHAT I DO HERE IN MY...
CHAMBER OF EXTREME KNITTING!

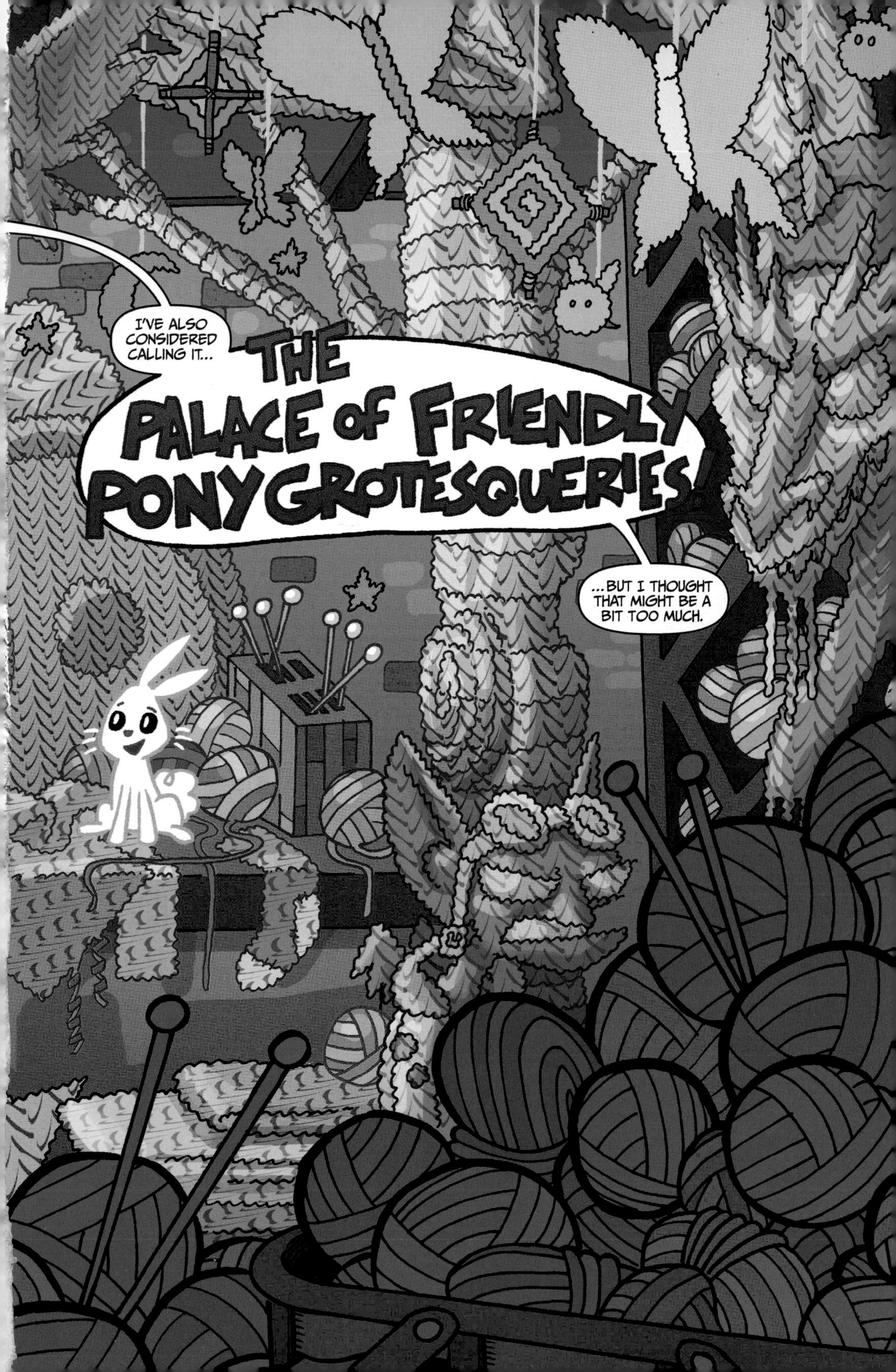
I'VE ALSO CONSIDERED CALLING IT...
THE PALACE of FRIENDLY PONY GROTESQUERIES!
...BUT I THOUGHT THAT MIGHT BE A BIT TOO MUCH.

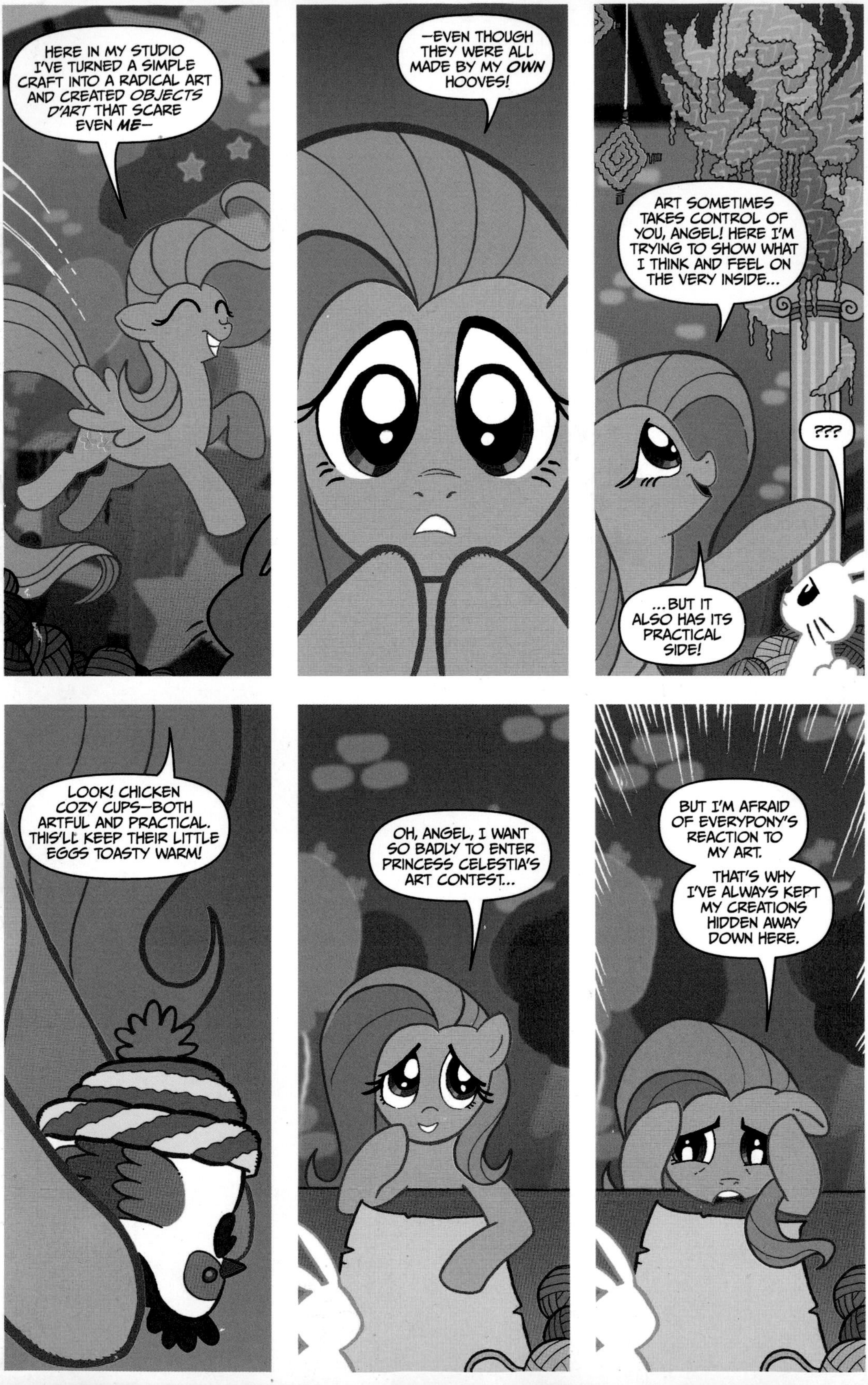
HERE IN MY STUDIO I'VE TURNED A SIMPLE CRAFT INTO A RADICAL ART AND CREATED OBJECTS D'ART THAT SCARE EVEN ME—
—EVEN THOUGH THEY WERE ALL MADE BY MY OWN HOOVES!
ART SOMETIMES TAKES CONTROL OF YOU, ANGEL! HERE I'M TRYING TO SHOW WHAT I THINK AND FEEL ON THE VERY INSIDE...
???
...BUT IT ALSO HAS ITS PRACTICAL SIDE!
LOOK! CHICKEN COZY CUPS—BOTH ARTFUL AND PRACTICAL. THIS'LL KEEP THEIR LITTLE EGGS TOASTY WARM!
OH, ANGEL, I WANT SO BADLY TO ENTER PRINCESS CELESTIA'S ART CONTEST...
BUT I'M AFRAID OF EVERYPONY'S REACTION TO MY ART.
THAT'S WHY I'VE ALWAYS KEPT MY CREATIONS HIDDEN AWAY DOWN HERE.

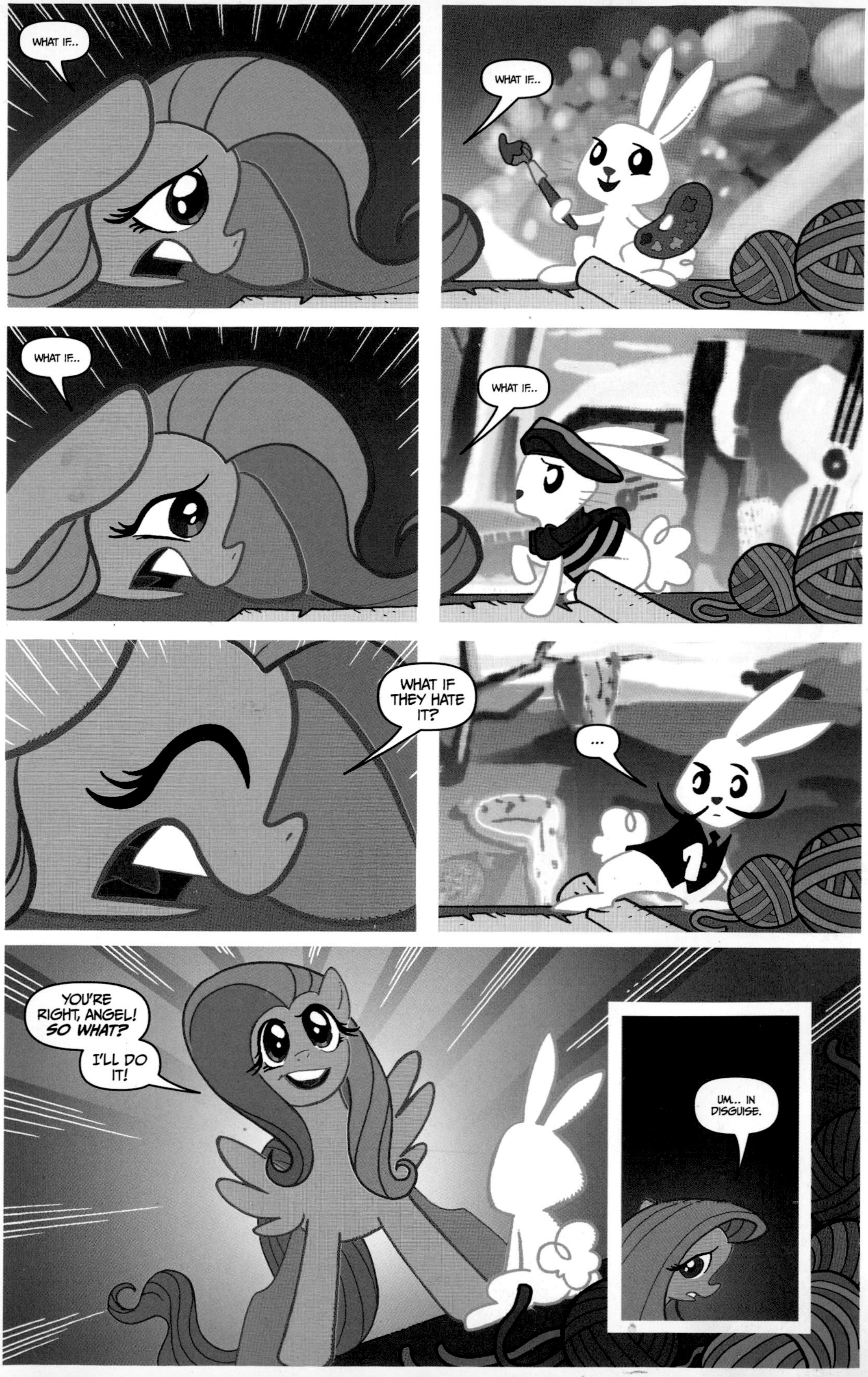
WHAT IF..
WHAT IF..
WHAT IF..
WHAT IF..
WHAT IF THEY HATE IT?
...
YOU'RE RIGHT, ANGEL! SO WHAT?
I'LL DO IT!
UM... IN DISGUISE.

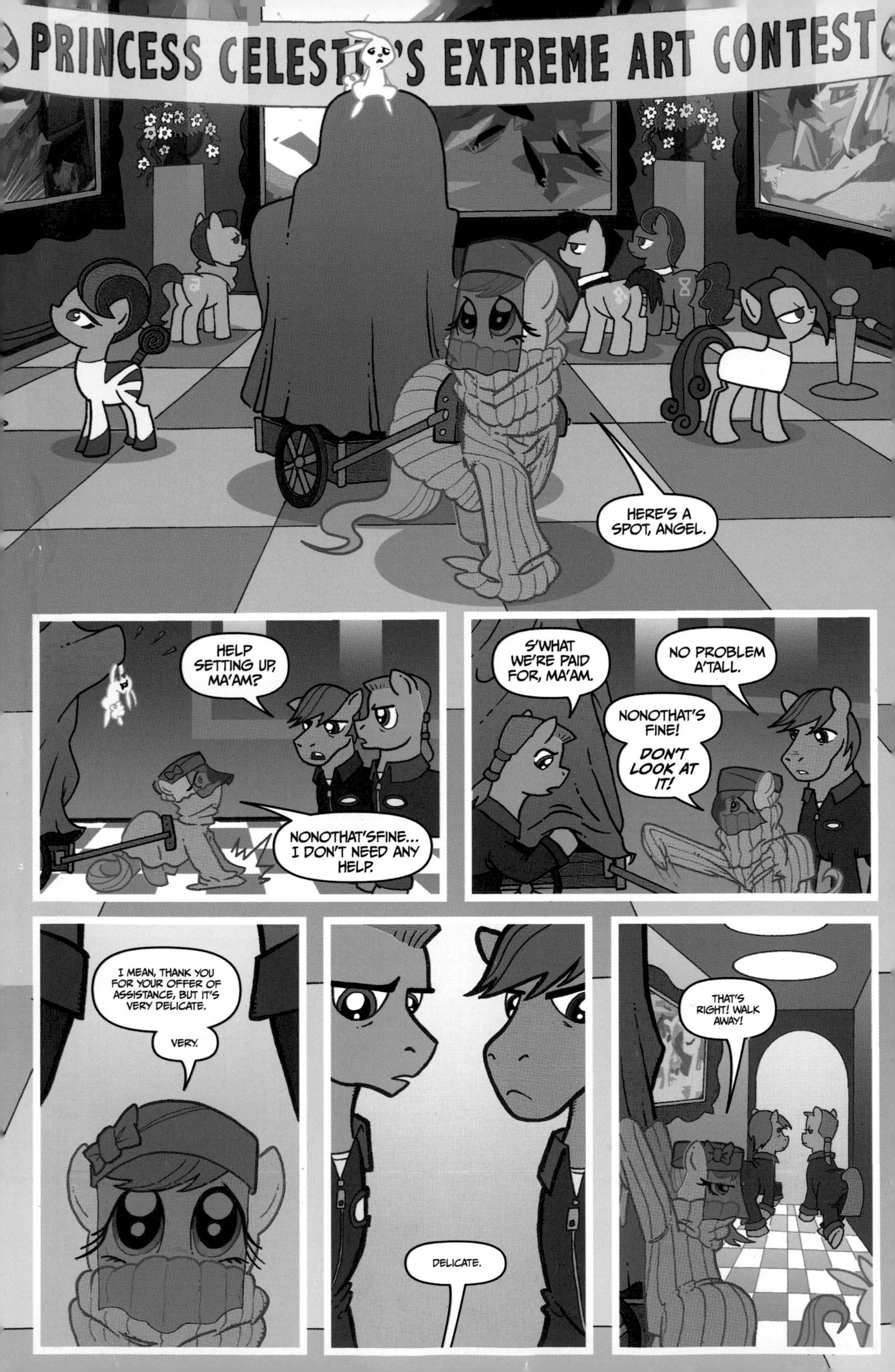
PRINCESS CELESTIA'S EXTREME ART CONTEST
HERE'S A SPOT, ANGEL.
HELP SETTING UP, MA'AM?
NONOTHAT'SFINE... I DON'T NEED ANY HELP.
S'WHAT WE'RE PAID FOR, MA'AM.
NO PROBLEM A'TALL.
NONOTHAT'S FINE!
DON'T LOOK AT IT!
I MEAN, THANK YOU FOR YOUR OFFER OF ASSISTANCE, BUT IT'S VERY DELICATE.
VERY.
DELICATE.
THAT'S RIGHT! WALK AWAY!

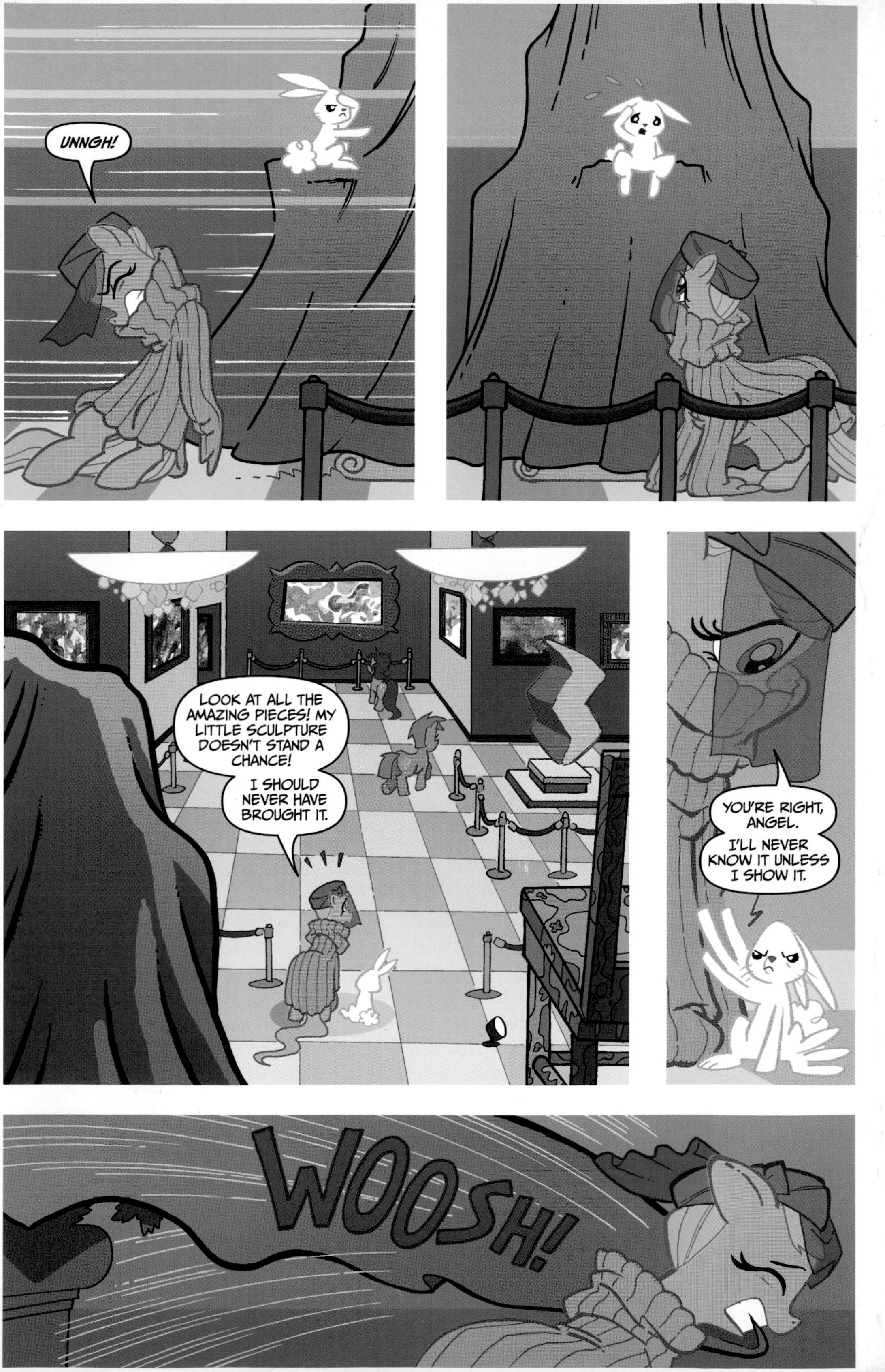
UNNGH!
LOOK AT ALL THE AMAZING PIECES! MY LITTLE SCULPTURE DOESN'T STAND A CHANCE!
I SHOULD NEVER HAVE BROUGHT IT.
YOU'RE RIGHT, ANGEL.
I'LL NEVER KNOW IT UNLESS I SHOW IT.
WOOSH!

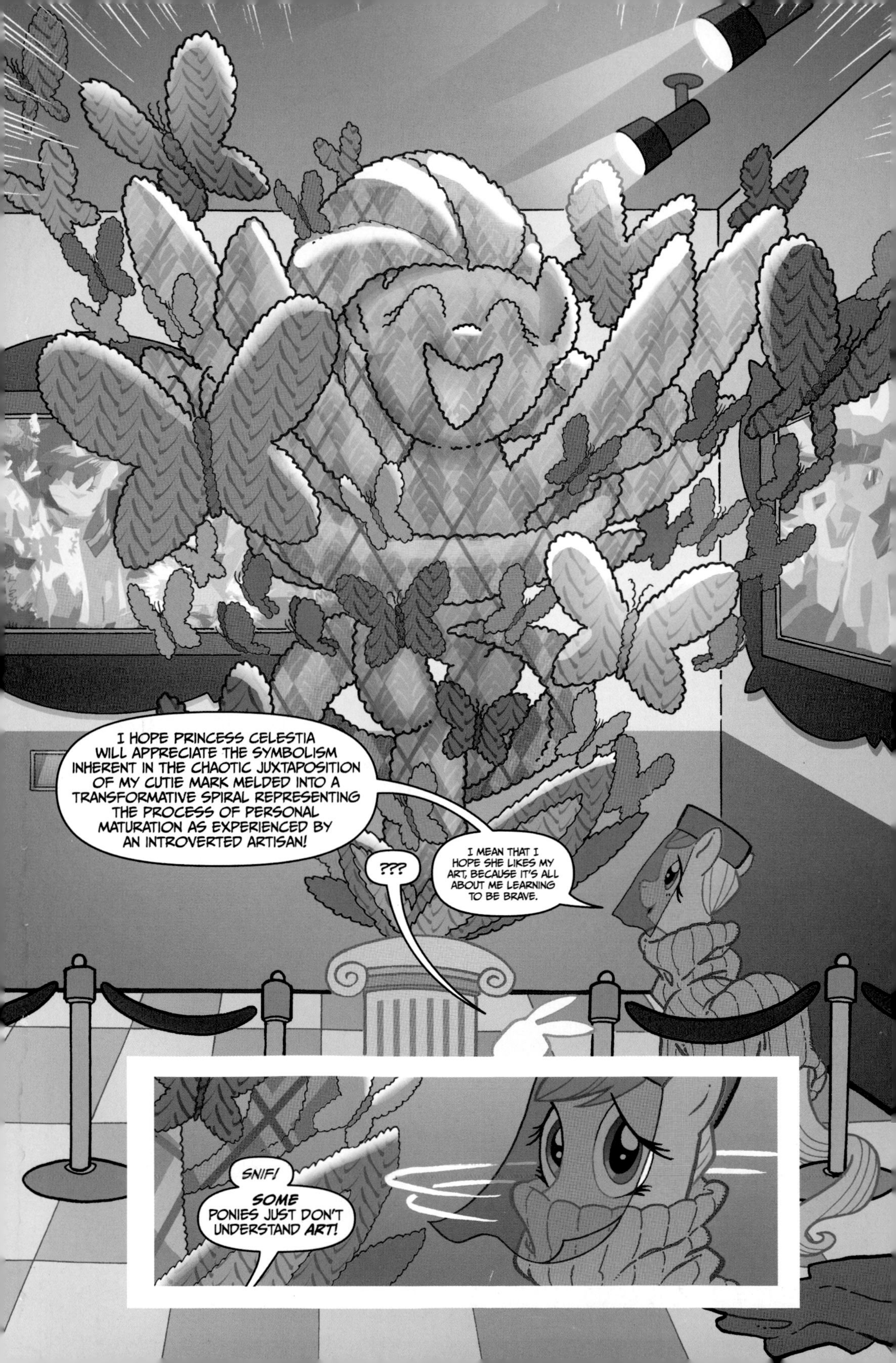
I HOPE PRINCESS CELESTIA WILL APPRECIATE THE SYMBOLISM INHERENT IN THE CHAOTIC JUXTAPOSITION OF MY CUTIE MARK MELDED INTO A TRANSFORMATIVE SPIRAL REPRESENTING THE PROCESS OF PERSONAL MATURATION AS EXPERIENCED BY AN INTROVERTED ARTISAN!
???
I MEAN THAT I HOPE SHE LIKES MY ART, BECAUSE IT'S ALL ABOUT ME LEARNING TO BE BRAVE.
SNIF!
SOME PONIES JUST DON'T UNDERSTAND ART!

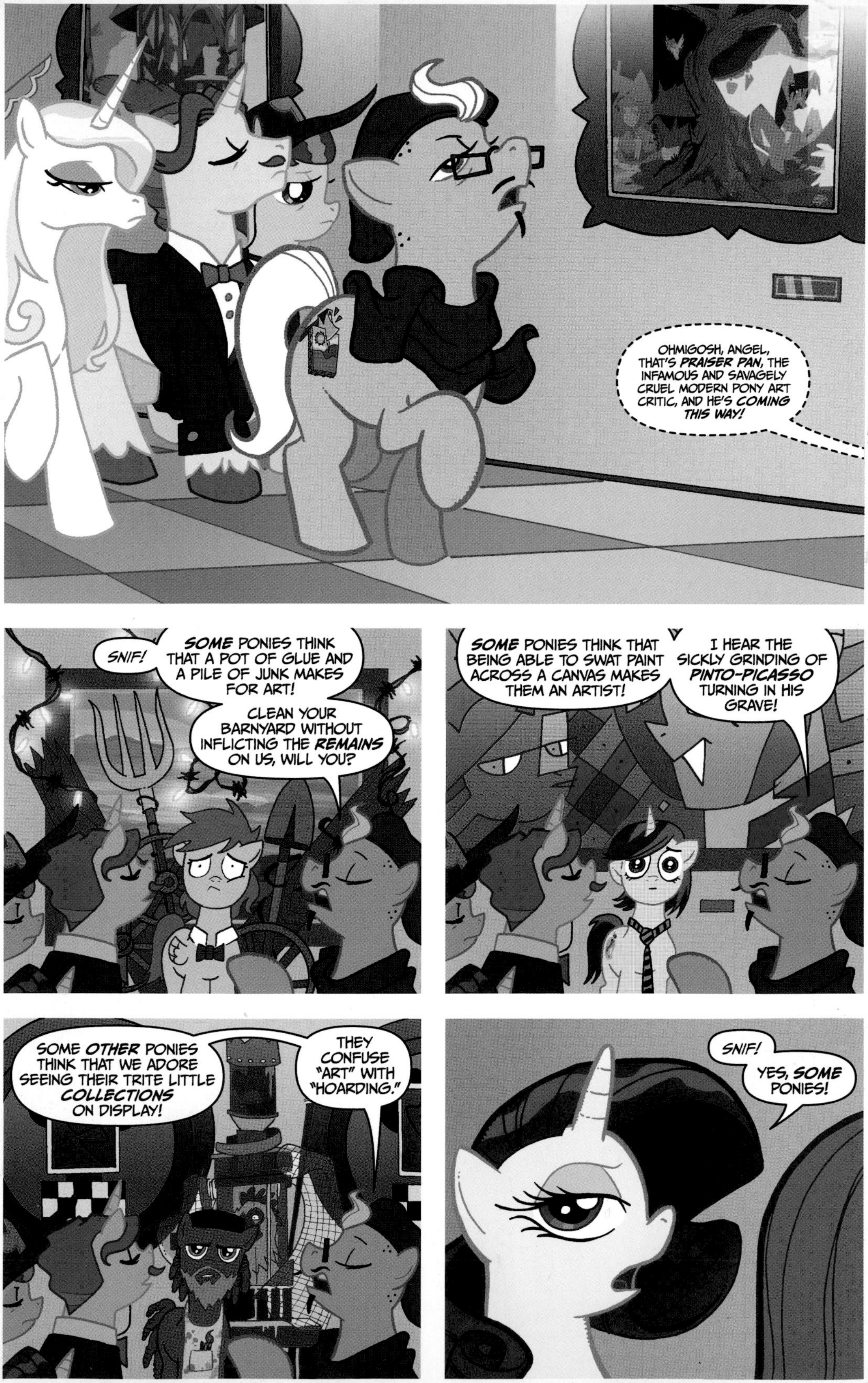
OHMIGOSH, ANGEL, THAT'S PRAISER PAN, THE INFAMOUS AND SAVAGELY CRUEL MODERN PONY ART CRITIC, AND HE'S COMING THIS WAY!
SNIF!
SOME PONIES THINK THAT A POT OF GLUE AND A PILE OF JUNK MAKES FOR ART!
CLEAN YOUR BARNYARD WITHOUT INFLICTING THE REMAINS ON US, WILL YOU?
SOME PONIES THINK THAT BEING ABLE TO SWAT PAINT ACROSS A CANVAS MAKES THEM AN ARTIST!
I HEAR THE SICKLY GRINDING OF PINTO-PICASSO TURNING IN HIS GRAVE!
SOME OTHER PONIES THINK THAT WE ADORE SEEING THEIR TRITE LITTLE COLLECTIONS ON DISPLAY!
THEY CONFUSE "ART" WITH "HOARDING."
SNIF!
YES, SOME PONIES!

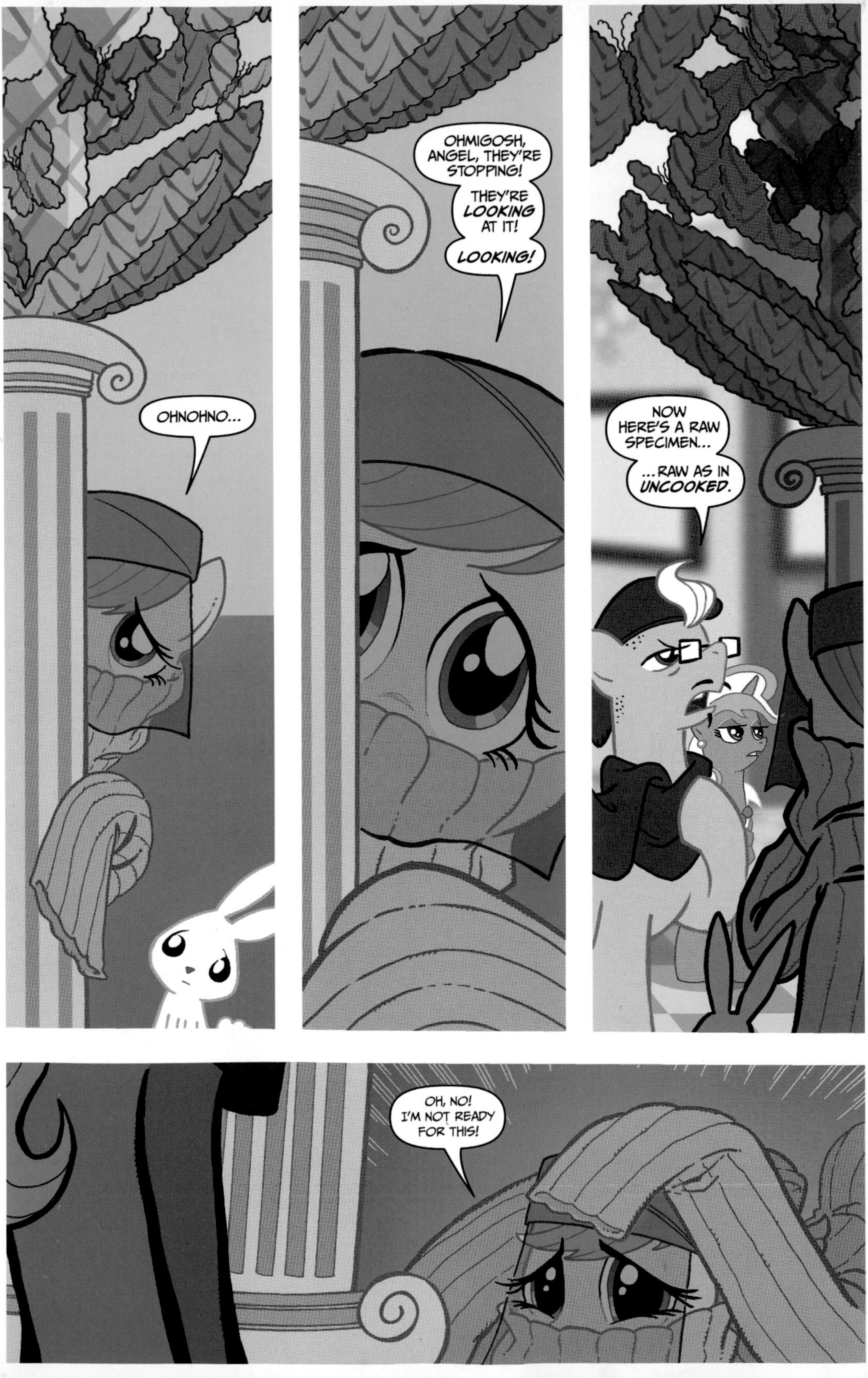
OHNOHNO...
OHMIGOSH, ANGEL, THEY'RE STOPPING!
THEY'RE *LOOKING* AT IT!
LOOKING!
NOW HERE'S A RAW SPECIMEN...
...RAW AS IN *UNCOOKED*.
OH, NO! I'M NOT READY FOR THIS!

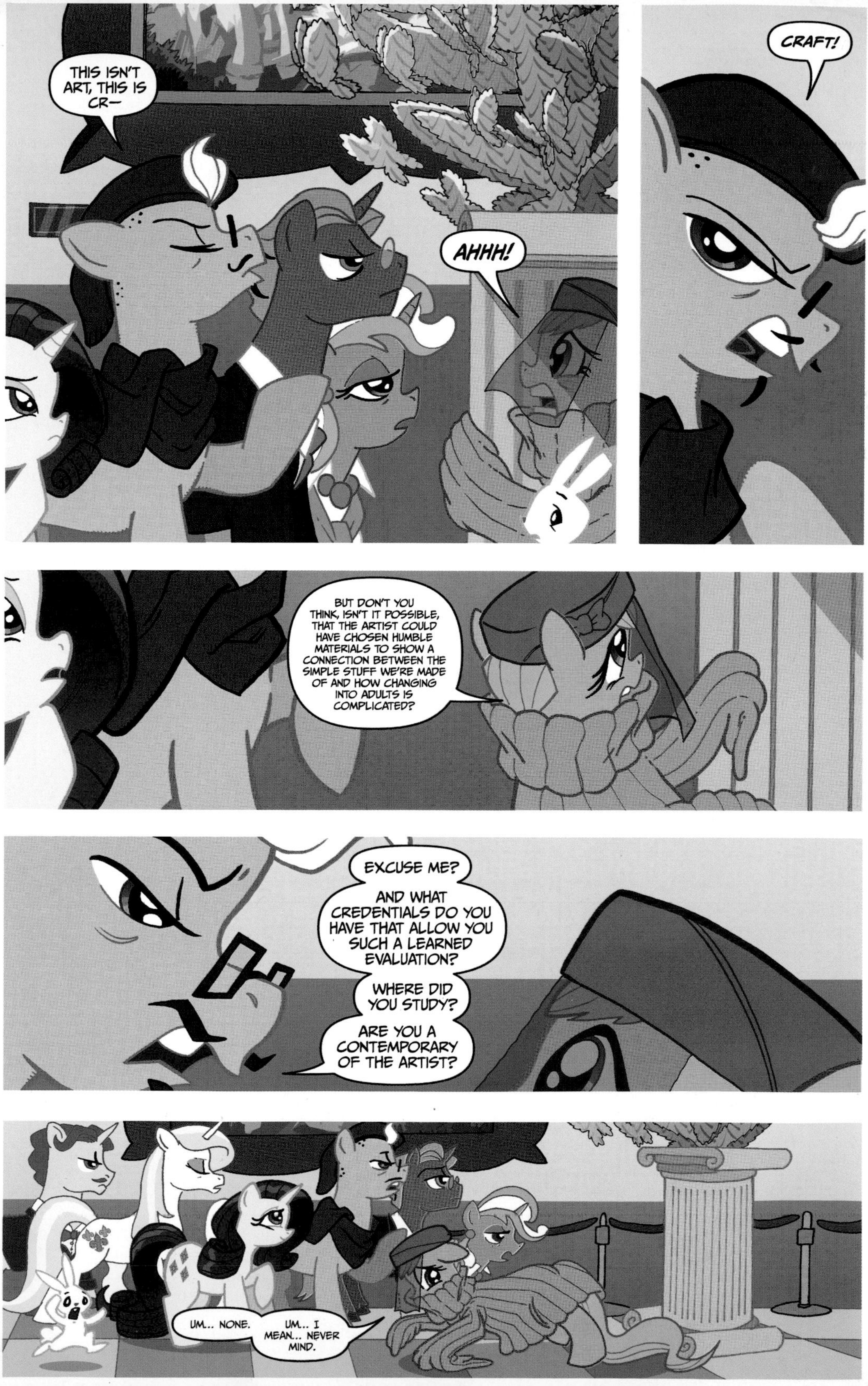
THIS ISN'T ART, THIS IS CR—
AHHH!
CRAFT!
BUT DON'T YOU THINK, ISN'T IT POSSIBLE, THAT THE ARTIST COULD HAVE CHOSEN HUMBLE MATERIALS TO SHOW A CONNECTION BETWEEN THE SIMPLE STUFF WE'RE MADE OF AND HOW CHANGING INTO ADULTS IS COMPLICATED?
EXCUSE ME?
AND WHAT CREDENTIALS DO YOU HAVE THAT ALLOW YOU SUCH A LEARNED EVALUATION?
WHERE DID YOU STUDY?
ARE YOU A CONTEMPORARY OF THE ARTIST?
UM... NONE.
UM... I MEAN... NEVER MIND.

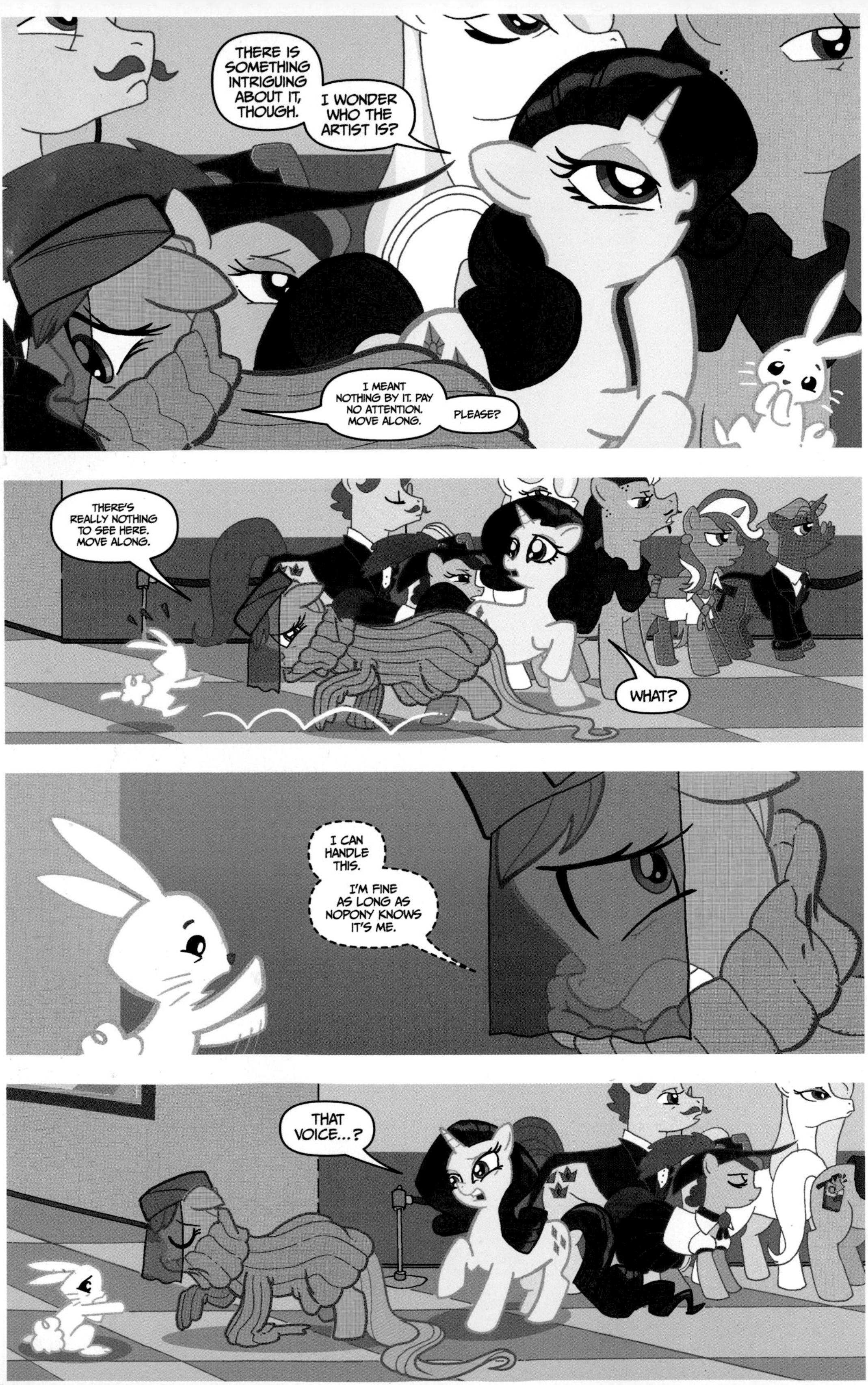
THERE IS SOMETHING INTRIGUING ABOUT IT, THOUGH.
I WONDER WHO THE ARTIST IS?
I MEANT NOTHING BY IT. PAY NO ATTENTION. MOVE ALONG.
PLEASE?
THERE'S REALLY NOTHING TO SEE HERE. MOVE ALONG.
WHAT?
I CAN HANDLE THIS.
I'M FINE AS LONG AS NOPONY KNOWS IT'S ME.
THAT VOICE...?

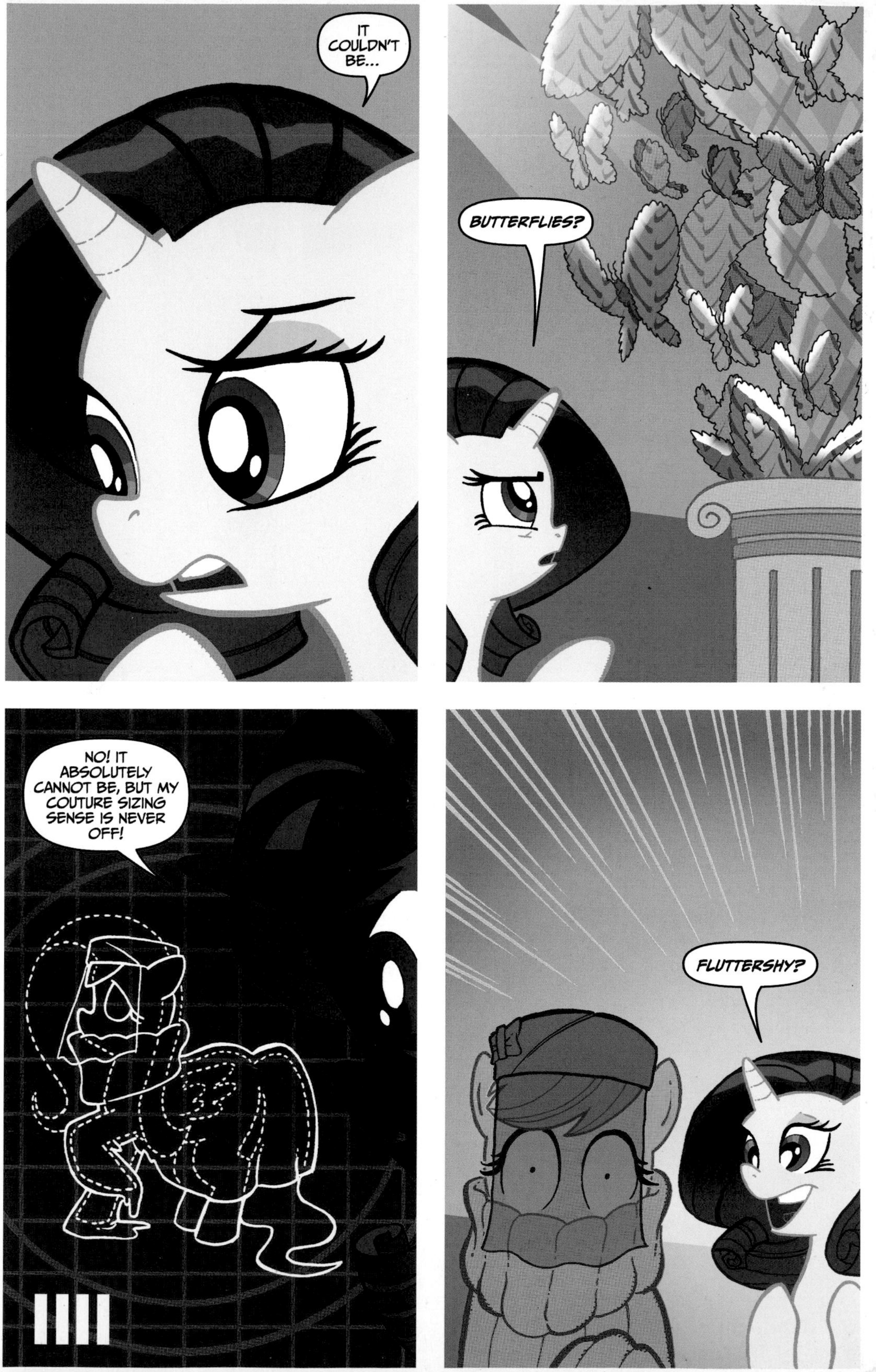
IT COULDN'T BE...
BUTTERFLIES?
NO! IT ABSOLUTELY CANNOT BE, BUT MY COUTURE SIZING SENSE IS NEVER OFF!
FLUTTERSHY?

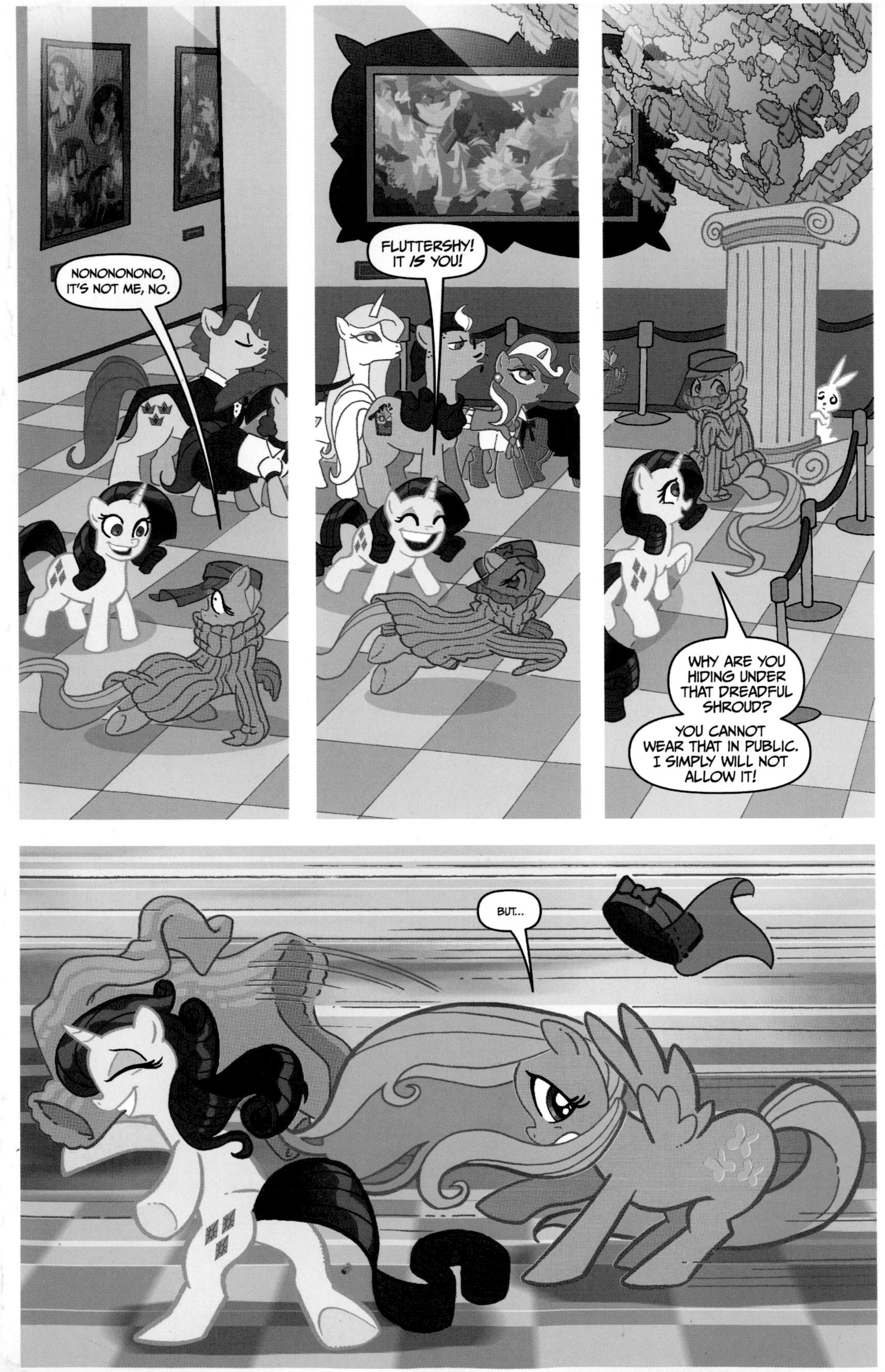
NONONONONO, IT'S NOT ME, NO.
FLUTTERSHY! IT IS YOU!
WHY ARE YOU HIDING UNDER THAT DREADFUL SHROUD?
YOU CANNOT WEAR THAT IN PUBLIC. I SIMPLY WILL NOT ALLOW IT!
BUT...

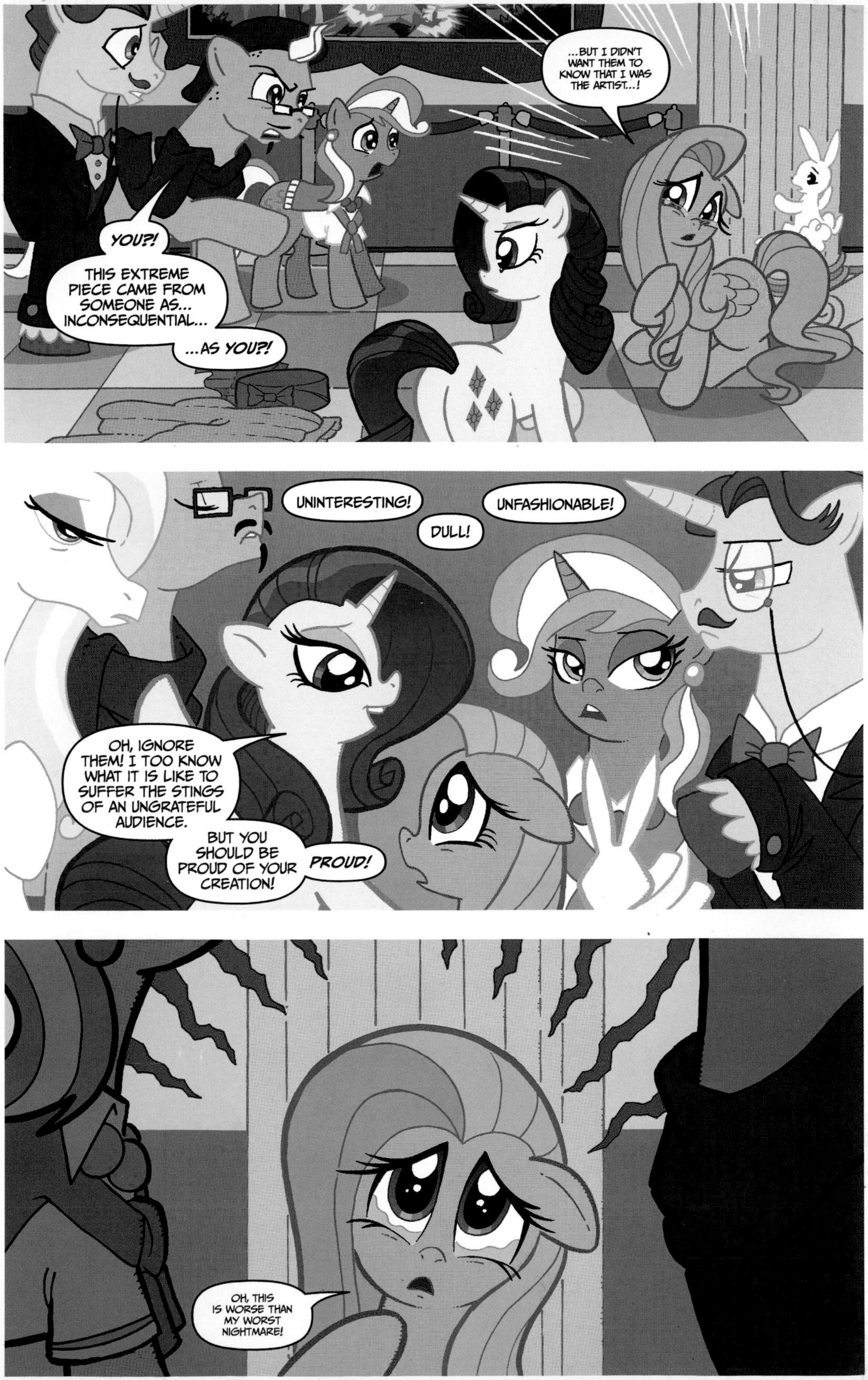
...BUT I DIDN'T WANT THEM TO KNOW THAT I WAS THE ARTIST...!
YOU?!
THIS EXTREME PIECE CAME FROM SOMEONE AS... INCONSEQUENTIAL...
...AS YOU?!
UNINTERESTING!
DULL!
UNFASHIONABLE!
OH, IGNORE THEM! I TOO KNOW WHAT IT IS LIKE TO SUFFER THE STINGS OF AN UNGRATEFUL AUDIENCE.
BUT YOU SHOULD BE PROUD OF YOUR CREATION!
PROUD!
OH, THIS IS WORSE THAN MY WORST NIGHTMARE!

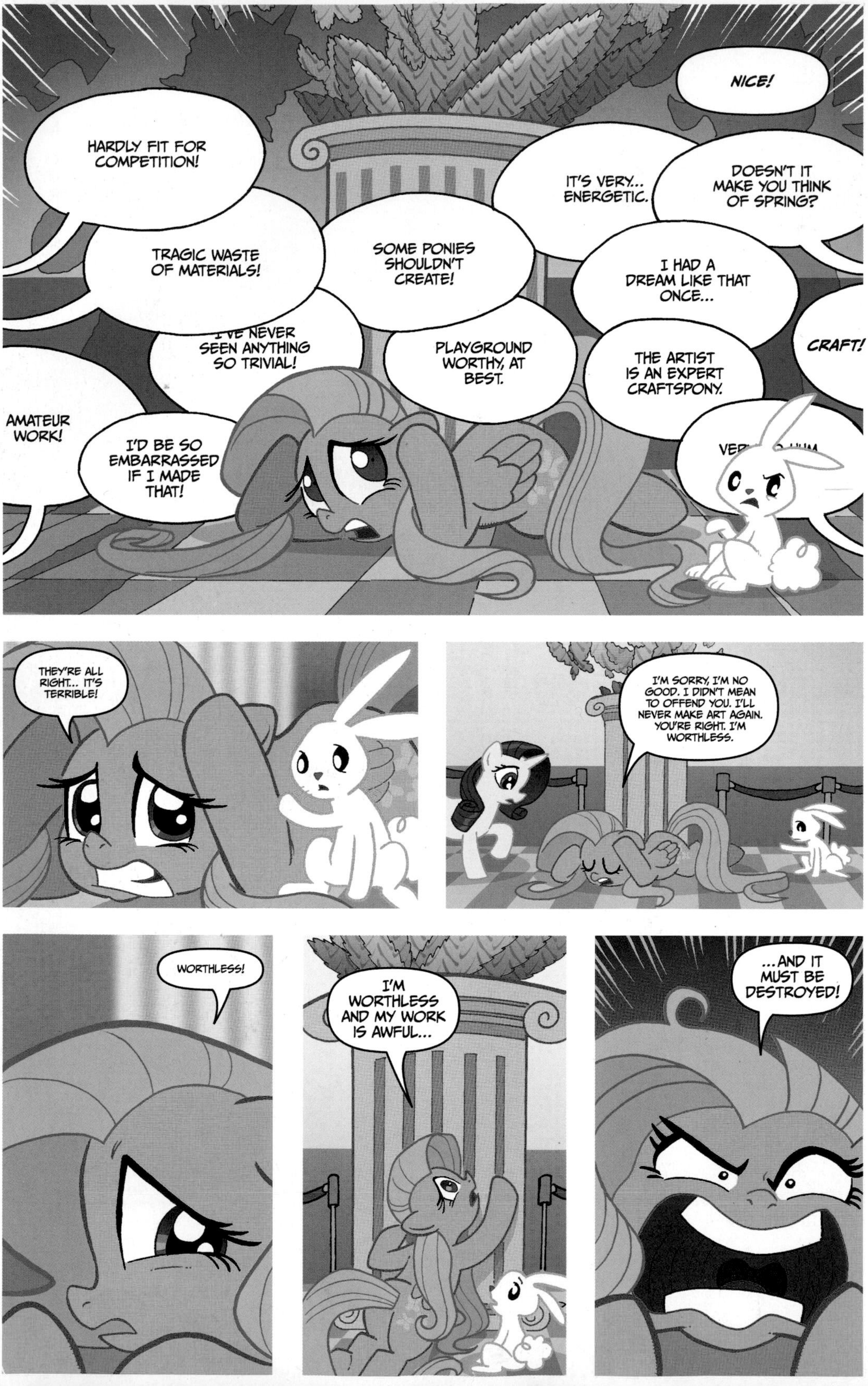
NICE!
HARDLY FIT FOR COMPETITION!
IT'S VERY... ENERGETIC.
DOESN'T IT MAKE YOU THINK OF SPRING?
TRAGIC WASTE OF MATERIALS!
SOME PONIES SHOULDN'T CREATE!
I HAD A DREAM LIKE THAT ONCE...
I'VE NEVER SEEN ANYTHING SO TRIVIAL!
PLAYGROUND WORTHY, AT BEST.
THE ARTIST IS AN EXPERT CRAFTSPONY.
CRAFT!
AMATEUR WORK!
I'D BE SO EMBARRASSED IF I MADE THAT!
THEY'RE ALL RIGHT... IT'S TERRIBLE!
I'M SORRY, I'M NO GOOD. I DIDN'T MEAN TO OFFEND YOU. I'LL NEVER MAKE ART AGAIN. YOU'RE RIGHT. I'M WORTHLESS.
WORTHLESS!
I'M WORTHLESS AND MY WORK IS AWFUL...
...AND IT MUST BE DESTROYED!

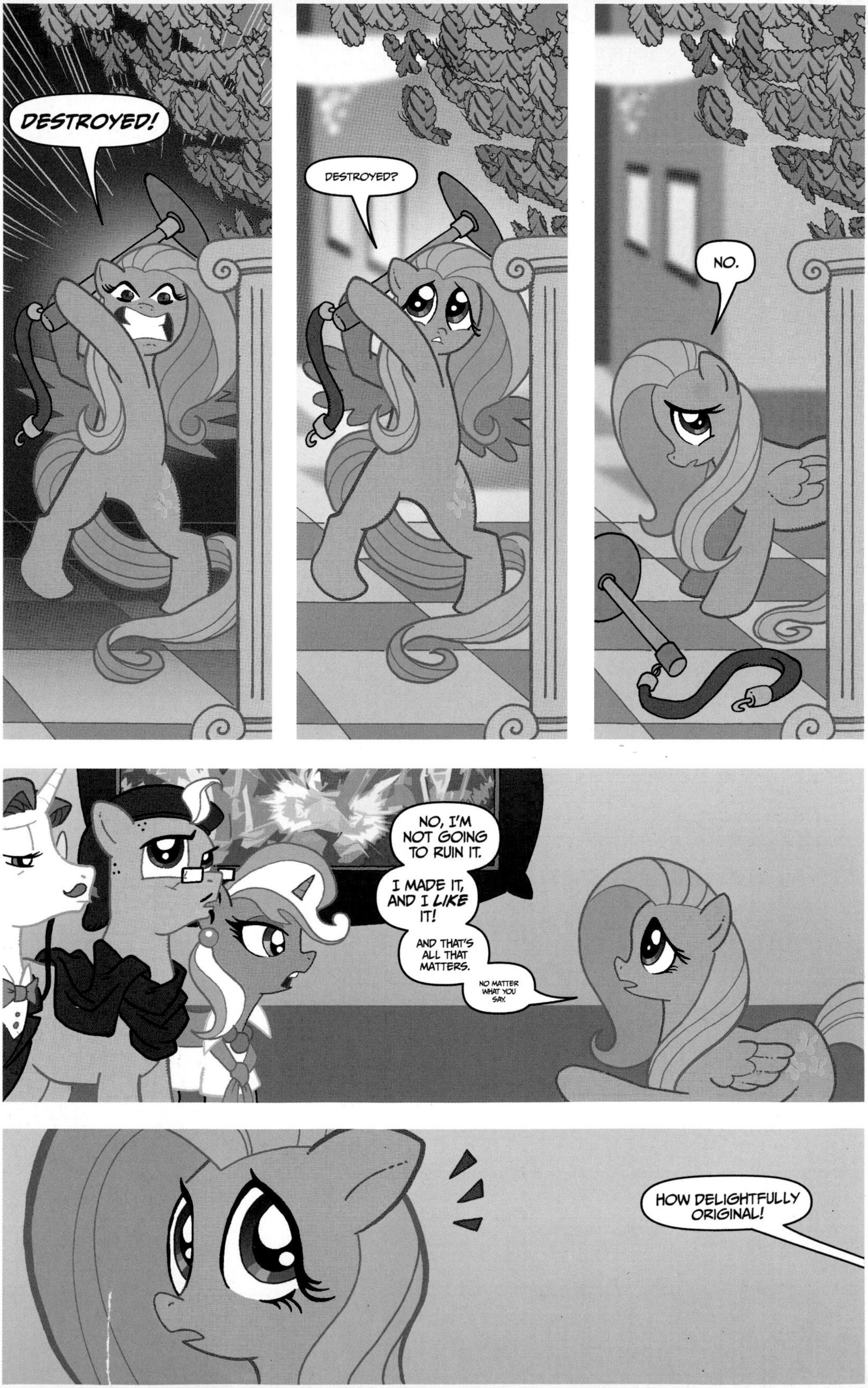
DESTROYED!
DESTROYED?
NO.
NO, I'M NOT GOING TO RUIN IT.
I MADE IT, AND I LIKE IT!
AND THAT'S ALL THAT MATTERS.
NO MATTER WHAT YOU SAY.
HOW DELIGHTFULLY ORIGINAL!

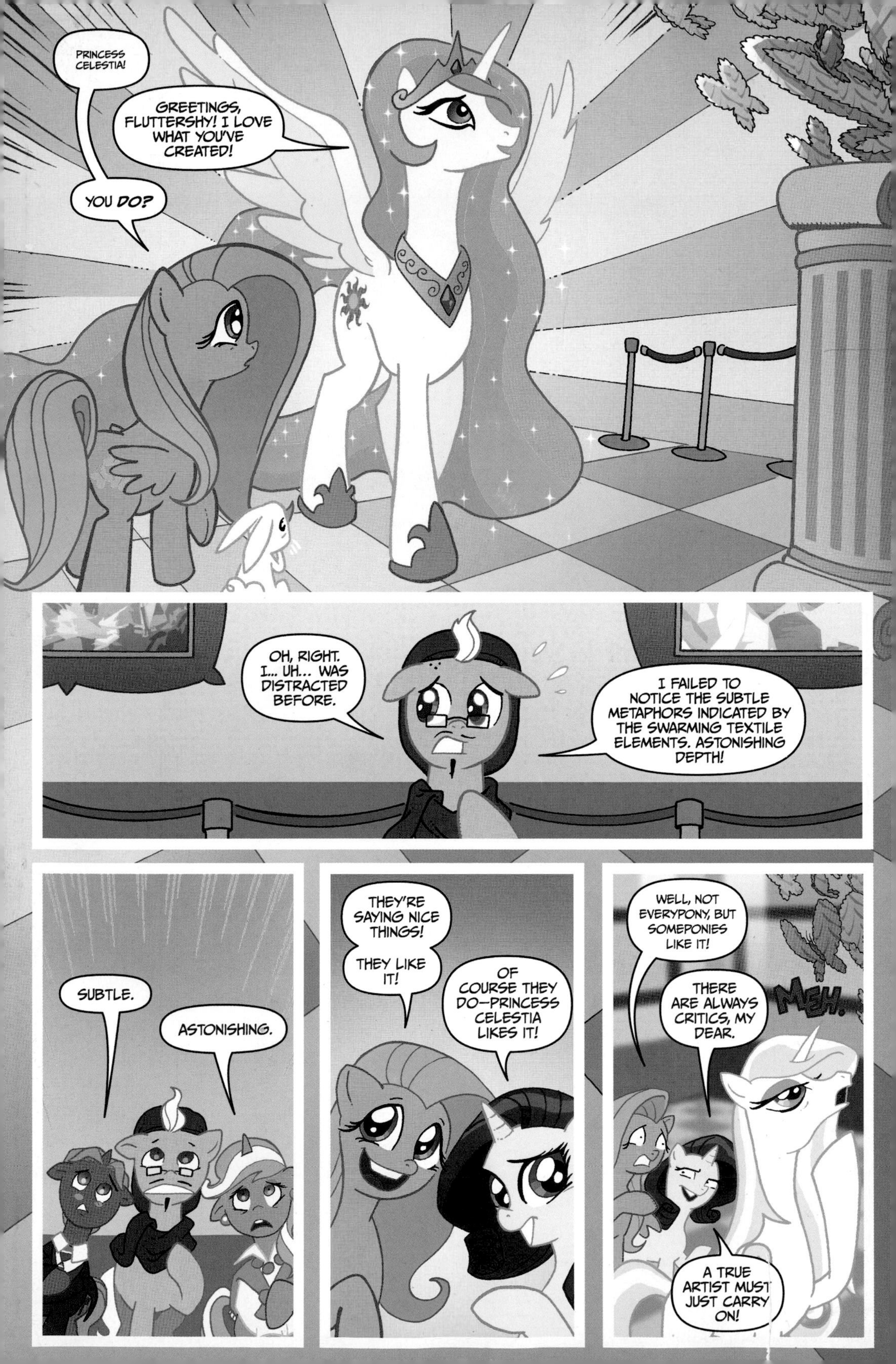
PRINCESS CELESTIA!
GREETINGS, FLUTTERSHY! I LOVE WHAT YOU'VE CREATED!
YOU *DO?*
OH, RIGHT. I... UH... WAS DISTRACTED BEFORE.
I FAILED TO NOTICE THE SUBTLE METAPHORS INDICATED BY THE SWARMING TEXTILE ELEMENTS. ASTONISHING DEPTH!
SUBTLE.
ASTONISHING.
THEY'RE SAYING NICE THINGS!
THEY LIKE IT!
OF COURSE THEY DO—PRINCESS CELESTIA LIKES IT!
WELL, NOT EVERYPONY, BUT SOMEPONIES LIKE IT!
MEH.
THERE ARE ALWAYS CRITICS, MY DEAR.
A TRUE ARTIST MUST JUST CARRY ON!

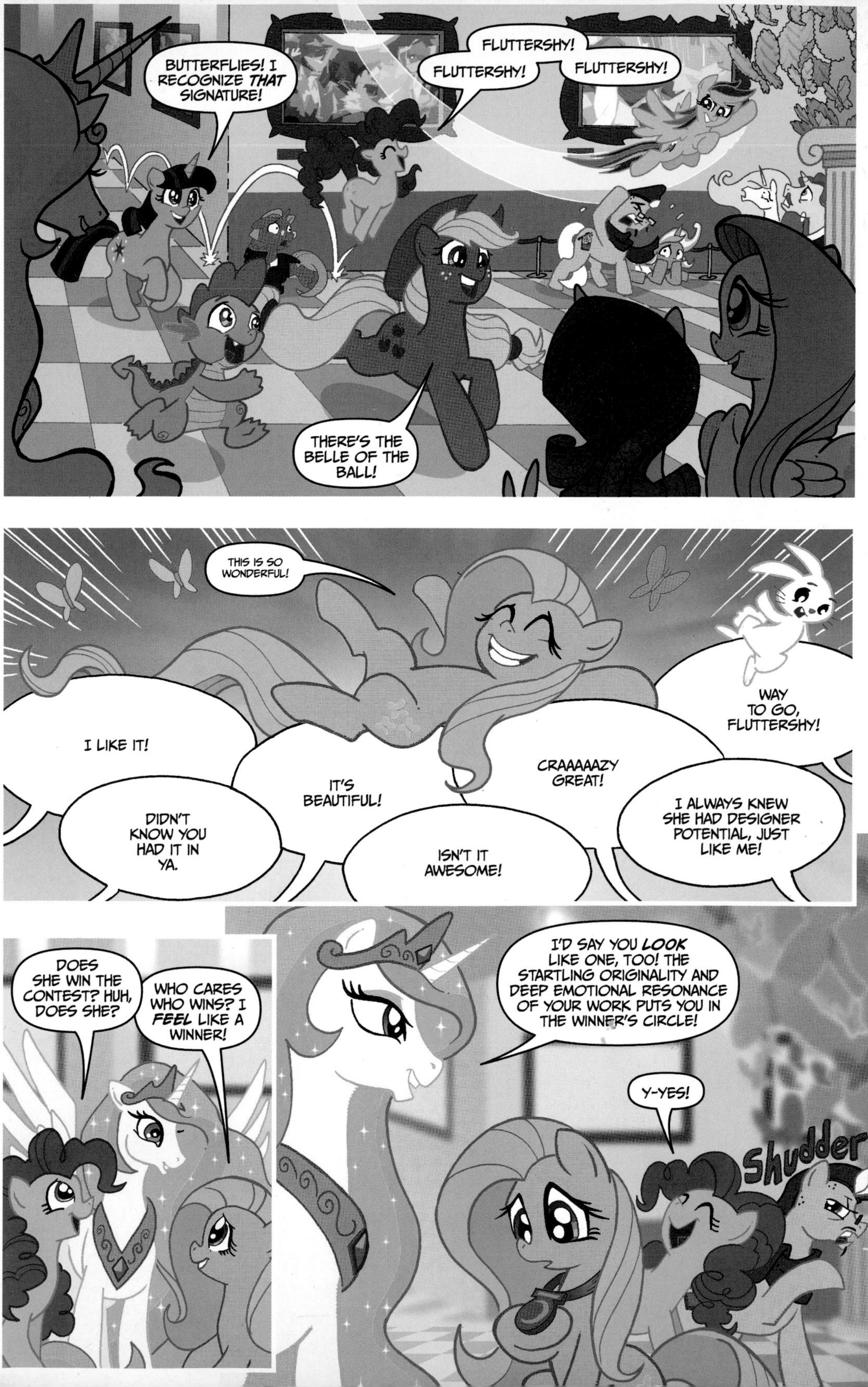
BUTTERFLIES! I RECOGNIZE *THAT* SIGNATURE!
FLUTTERSHY!
FLUTTERSHY!
FLUTTERSHY!
THERE'S THE BELLE OF THE BALL!
THIS IS SO WONDERFUL!
I LIKE IT!
DIDN'T KNOW YOU HAD IT IN YA.
IT'S BEAUTIFUL!
ISN'T IT AWESOME!
CRAAAAAZY GREAT!
WAY TO GO, FLUTTERSHY!
I ALWAYS KNEW SHE HAD DESIGNER POTENTIAL, JUST LIKE ME!
DOES SHE WIN THE CONTEST? HUH, DOES SHE?
WHO CARES WHO WINS? I *FEEL* LIKE A WINNER!
I'D SAY YOU *LOOK* LIKE ONE, TOO! THE STARTLING ORIGINALITY AND DEEP EMOTIONAL RESONANCE OF YOUR WORK PUTS YOU IN THE WINNER'S CIRCLE!
Y-YES!
Shudder

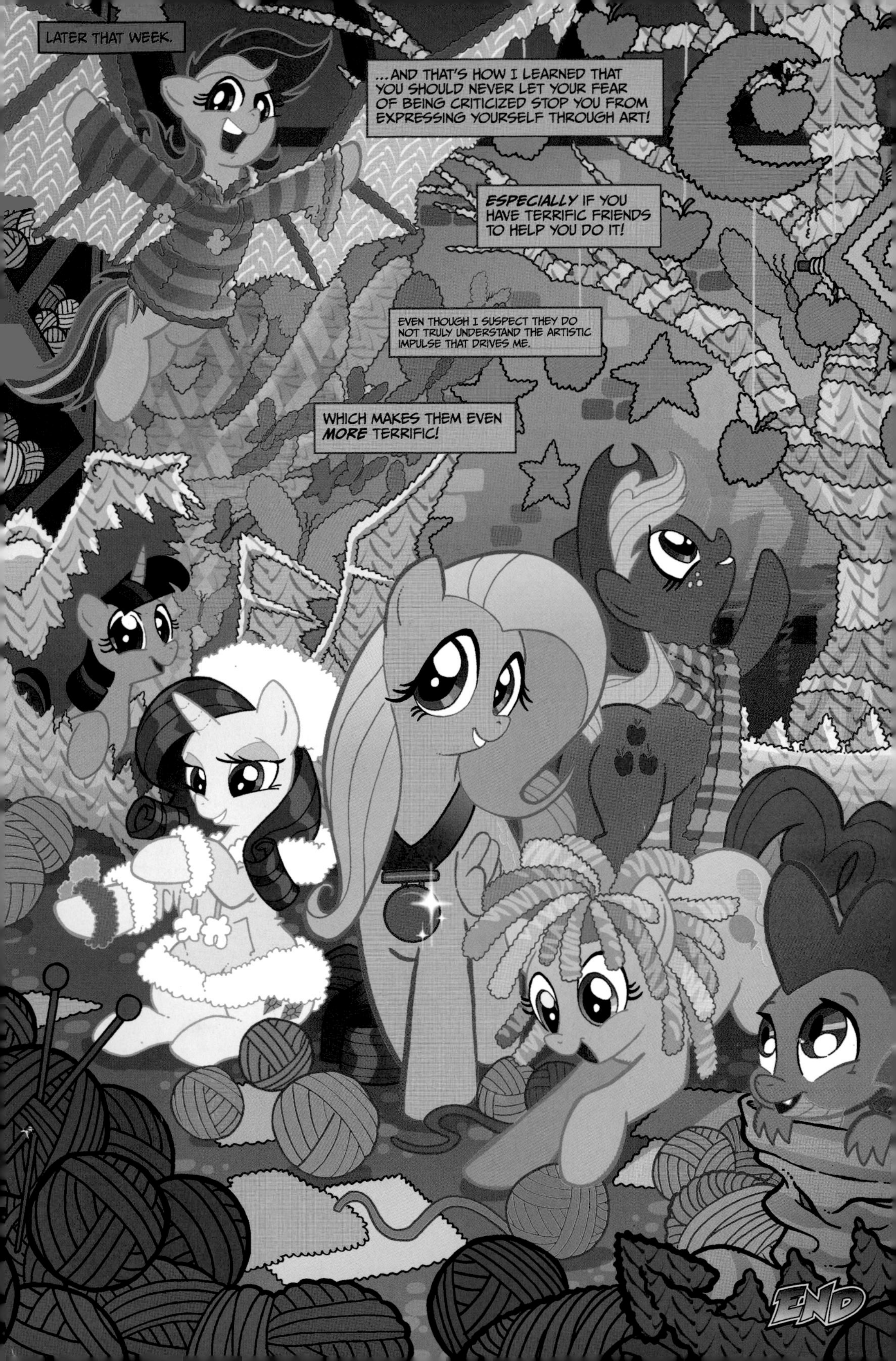
LATER THAT WEEK.
...AND THAT'S HOW I LEARNED THAT YOU SHOULD NEVER LET YOUR FEAR OF BEING CRITICIZED STOP YOU FROM EXPRESSING YOURSELF THROUGH ART!
ESPECIALLY IF YOU HAVE TERRIFIC FRIENDS TO HELP YOU DO IT!
EVEN THOUGH I SUSPECT THEY DO NOT TRULY UNDERSTAND THE ARTISTIC IMPULSE THAT DRIVES ME.
WHICH MAKES THEM EVEN *MORE* TERRIFIC!
END

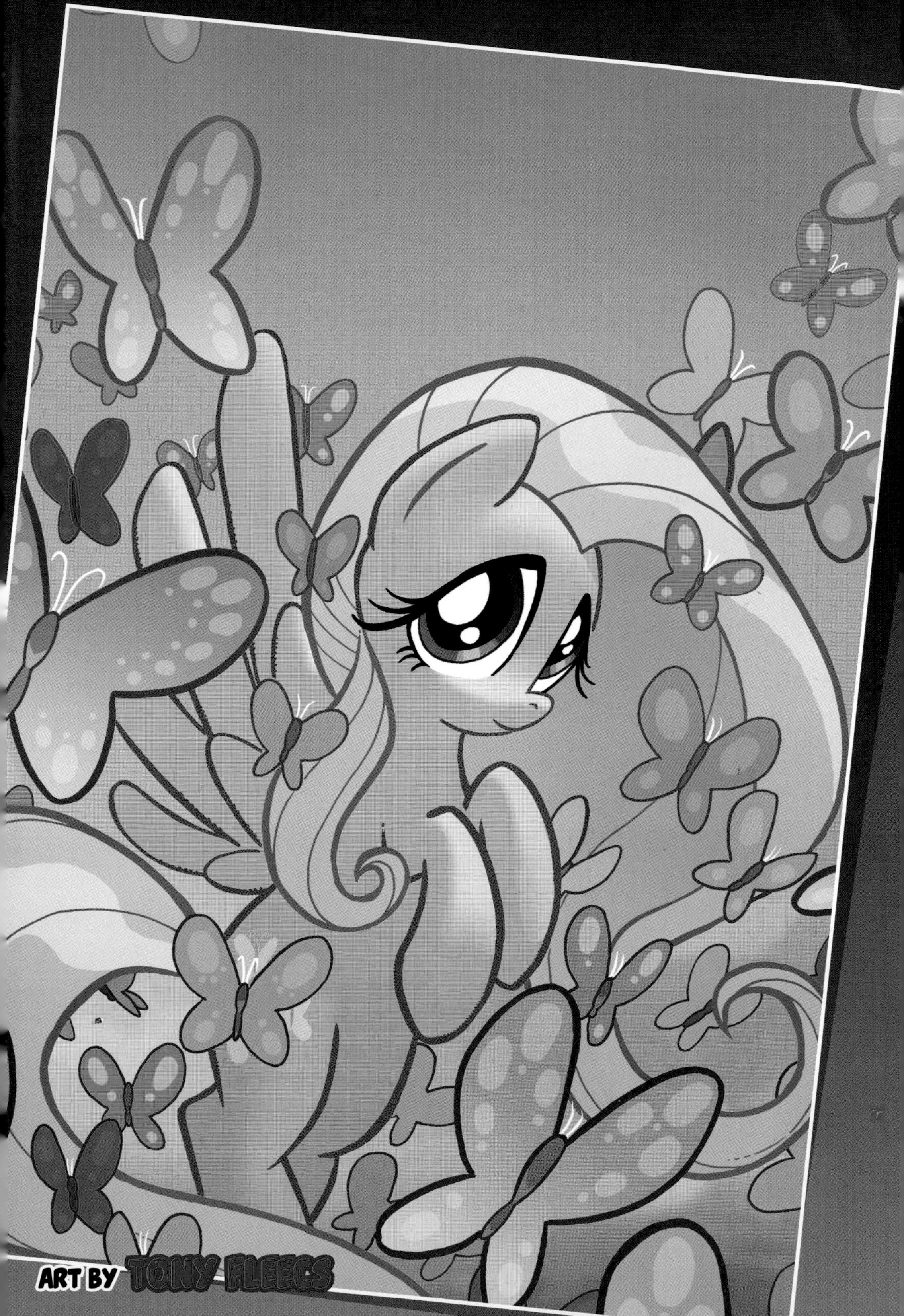
ART BY TONY FLEECS

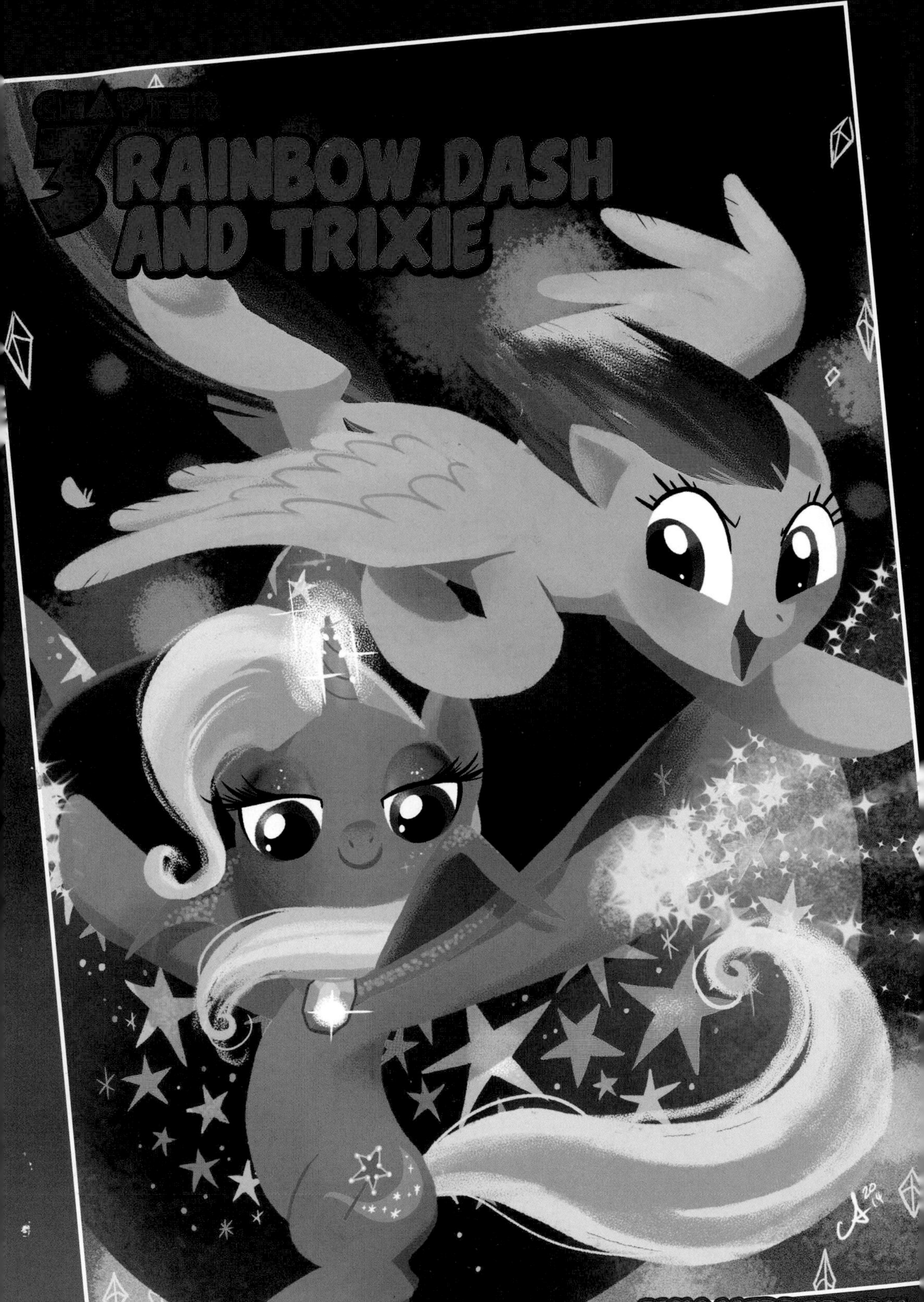
CHAPTER 3
RAINBOW DASH AND TRIXIE
ART BY AMY MEBBERSON

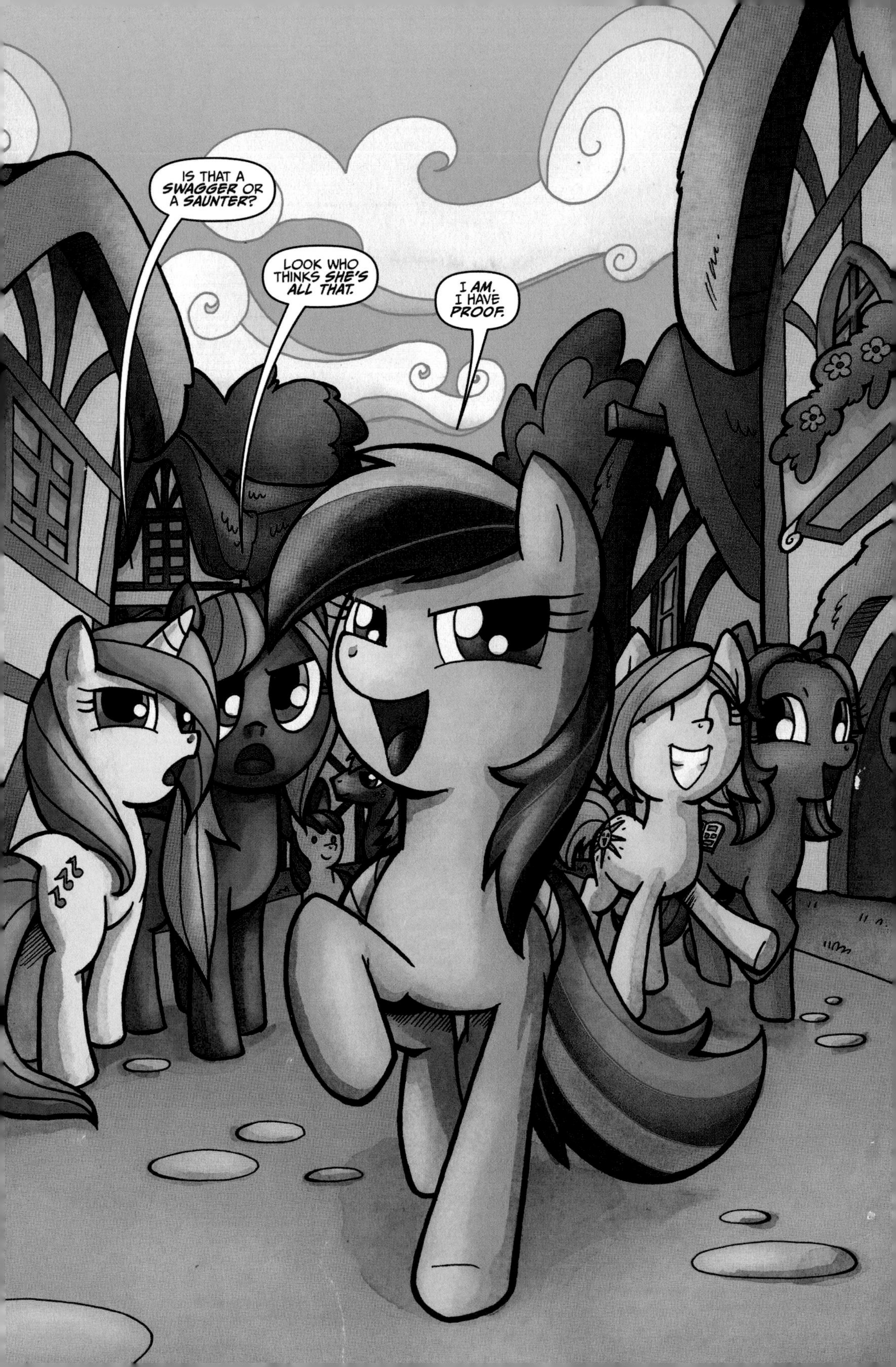
IS THAT A SWAGGER OR A SAUNTER?
LOOK WHO THINKS SHE'S ALL THAT.
I AM. I HAVE PROOF.

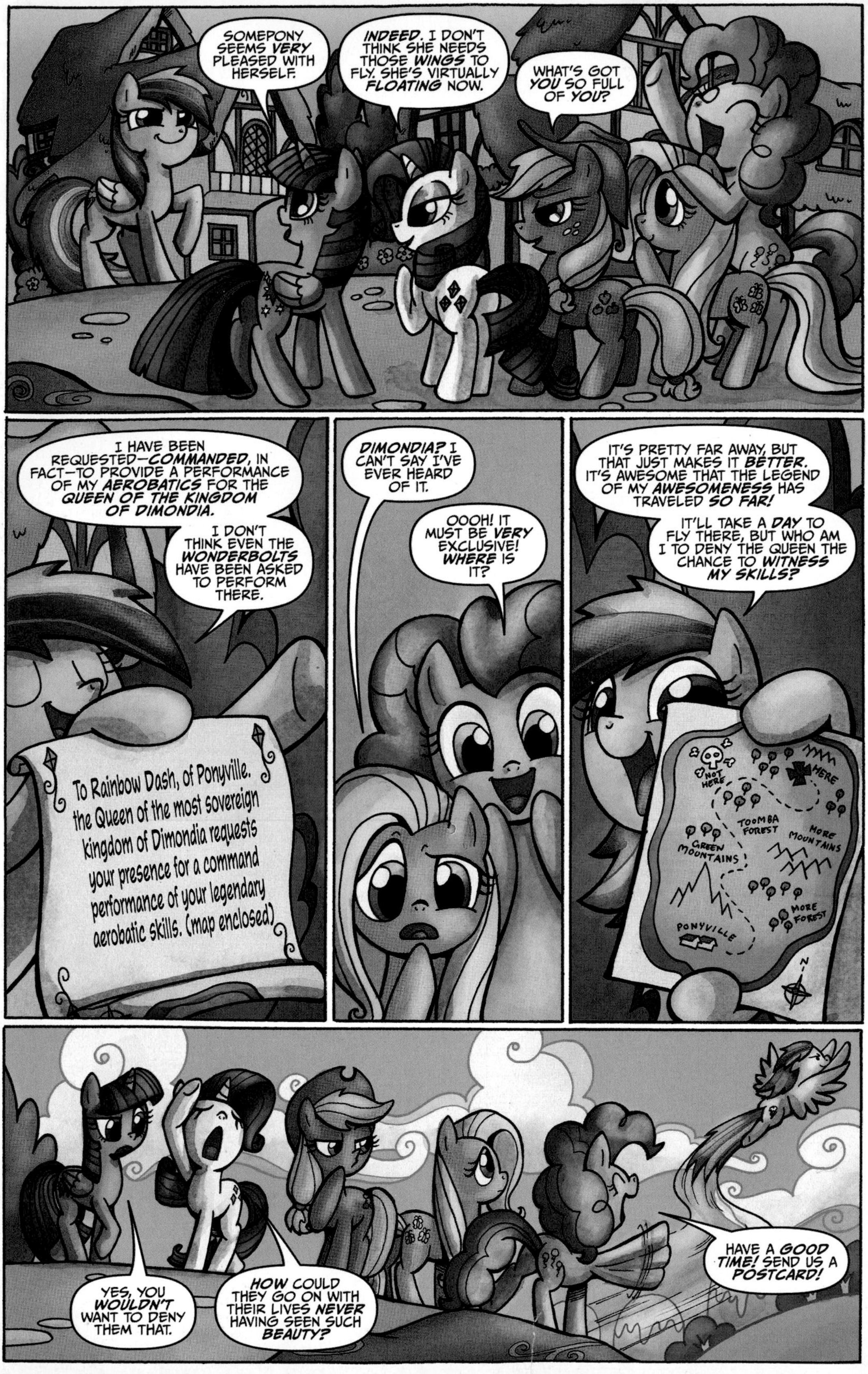
SOMEPONY SEEMS VERY PLEASED WITH HERSELF.
INDEED. I DON'T THINK SHE NEEDS THOSE WINGS TO FLY. SHE'S VIRTUALLY FLOATING NOW.
WHAT'S GOT YOU SO FULL OF YOU?
I HAVE BEEN REQUESTED—COMMANDED, IN FACT—TO PROVIDE A PERFORMANCE OF MY AEROBATICS FOR THE QUEEN OF THE KINGDOM OF DIMONDIA.
I DON'T THINK EVEN THE WONDERBOLTS HAVE BEEN ASKED TO PERFORM THERE.
To Rainbow Dash, of Ponyville. the Queen of the most sovereign kingdom of Dimondia requests your presence for a command performance of your legendary aerobatic skills. (map enclosed)
DIMONDIA? I CAN'T SAY I'VE EVER HEARD OF IT.
OOOH! IT MUST BE VERY EXCLUSIVE! WHERE IS IT?
IT'S PRETTY FAR AWAY, BUT THAT JUST MAKES IT BETTER. IT'S AWESOME THAT THE LEGEND OF MY AWESOMENESS HAS TRAVELED SO FAR!
IT'LL TAKE A DAY TO FLY THERE, BUT WHO AM I TO DENY THE QUEEN THE CHANCE TO WITNESS MY SKILLS?
NOT HERE
HERE
TOOMBA FOREST
MORE MOUNTAINS
GREEN MOUNTAINS
MORE FOREST
PONYVILLE
N
YES, YOU WOULDN'T WANT TO DENY THEM THAT.
HOW COULD THEY GO ON WITH THEIR LIVES NEVER HAVING SEEN SUCH BEAUTY?
HAVE A GOOD TIME! SEND US A POSTCARD!

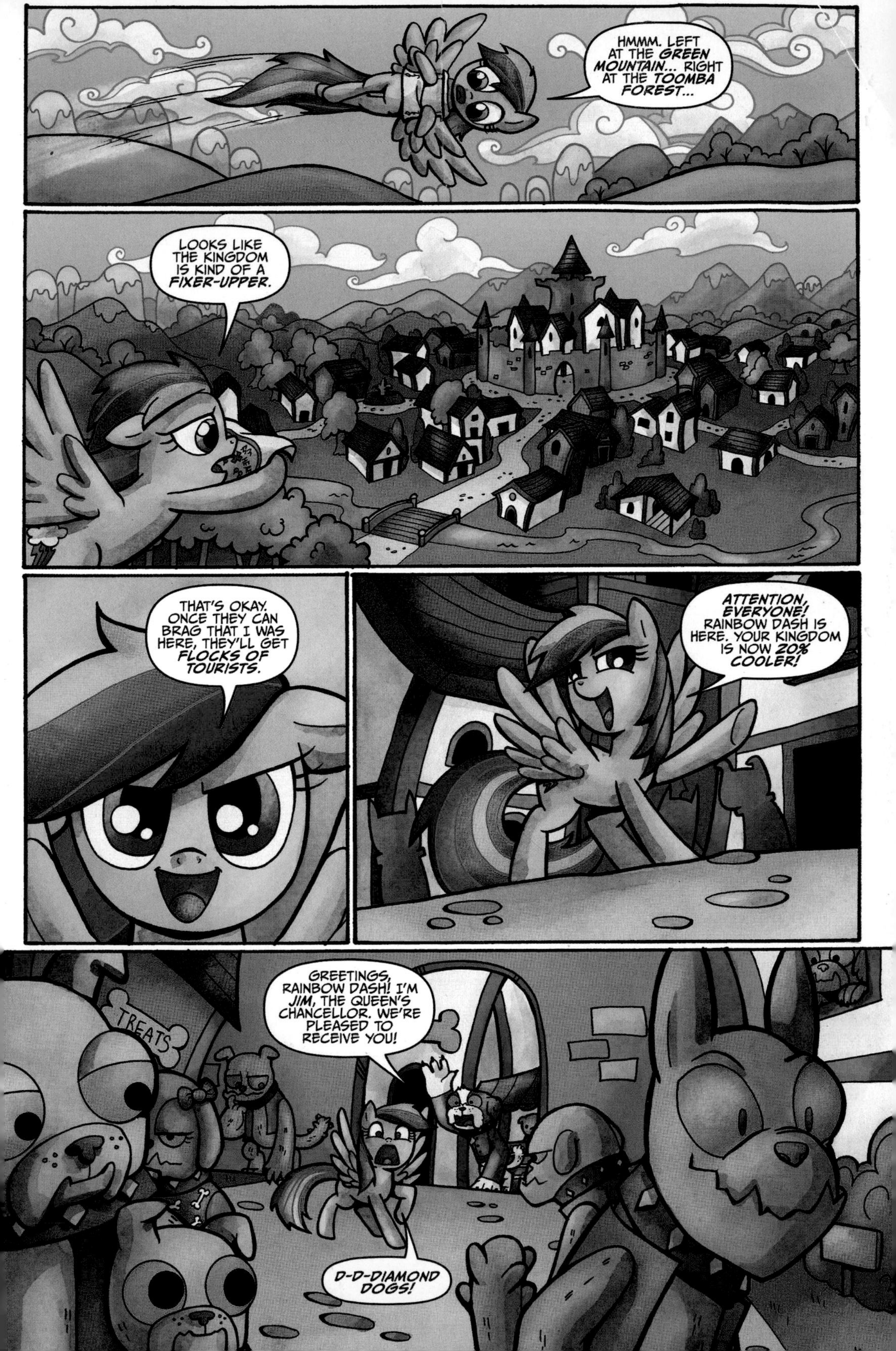
HMMM. LEFT AT THE GREEN MOUNTAIN... RIGHT AT THE TOOMBA FOREST...
LOOKS LIKE THE KINGDOM IS KIND OF A FIXER-UPPER.
THAT'S OKAY. ONCE THEY CAN BRAG THAT I WAS HERE, THEY'LL GET FLOCKS OF TOURISTS.
ATTENTION, EVERYONE! RAINBOW DASH IS HERE. YOUR KINGDOM IS NOW 20% COOLER!
TREATS
GREETINGS, RAINBOW DASH! I'M JIM, THE QUEEN'S CHANCELLOR. WE'RE PLEASED TO RECEIVE YOU!
D-D-DIAMOND DOGS!

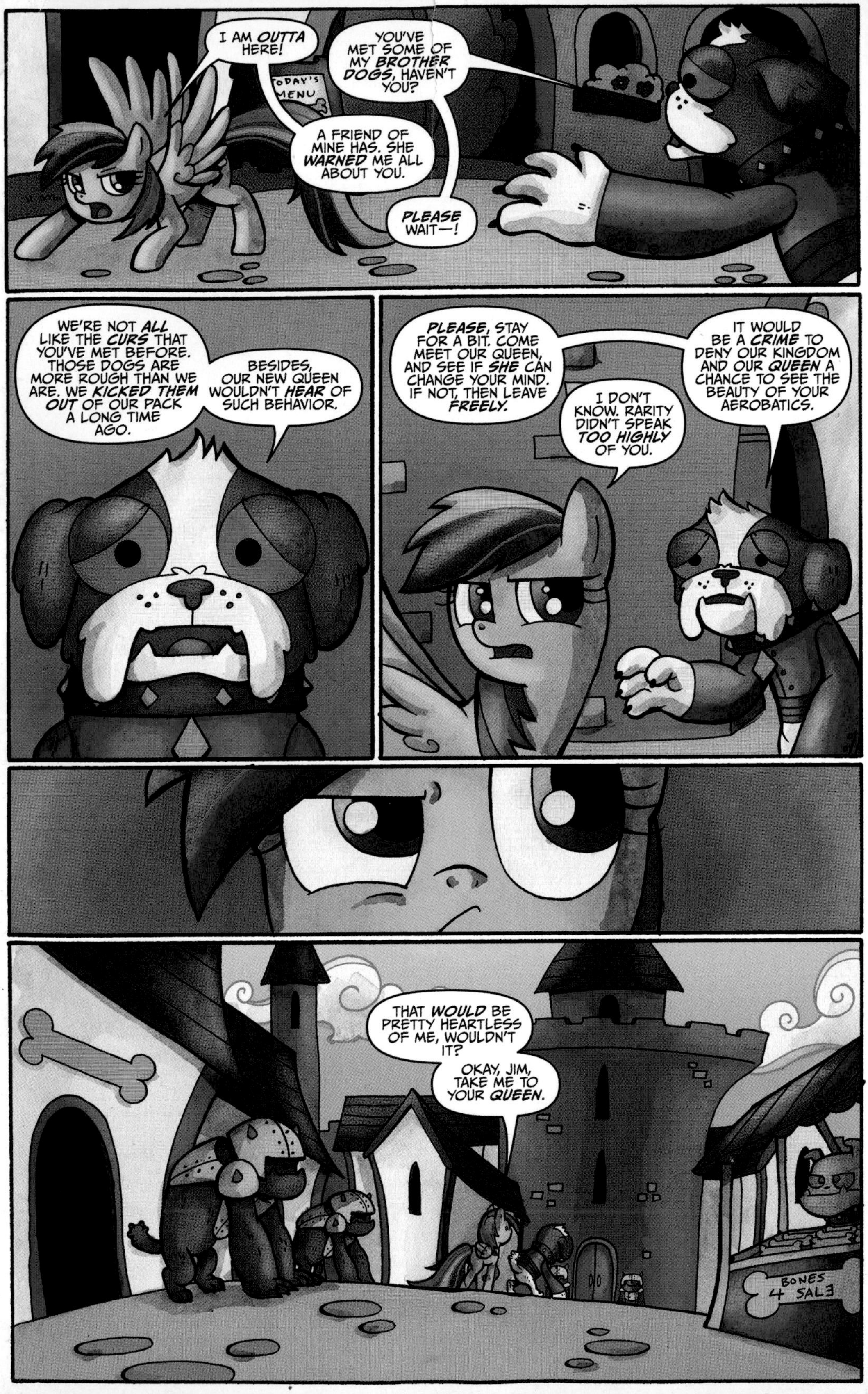
I AM OUTTA HERE!
YOU'VE MET SOME OF MY BROTHER DOGS, HAVEN'T YOU?
A FRIEND OF MINE HAS. SHE WARNED ME ALL ABOUT YOU.
PLEASE WAIT—!
TODAY'S MENU
WE'RE NOT ALL LIKE THE CURS THAT YOU'VE MET BEFORE. THOSE DOGS ARE MORE ROUGH THAN WE ARE. WE KICKED THEM OUT OF OUR PACK A LONG TIME AGO.
BESIDES, OUR NEW QUEEN WOULDN'T HEAR OF SUCH BEHAVIOR.
PLEASE, STAY FOR A BIT. COME MEET OUR QUEEN, AND SEE IF SHE CAN CHANGE YOUR MIND. IF NOT, THEN LEAVE FREELY.
IT WOULD BE A CRIME TO DENY OUR KINGDOM AND OUR QUEEN A CHANCE TO SEE THE BEAUTY OF YOUR AEROBATICS.
I DON'T KNOW. RARITY DIDN'T SPEAK TOO HIGHLY OF YOU.
THAT WOULD BE PRETTY HEARTLESS OF ME, WOULDN'T IT?
OKAY, JIM, TAKE ME TO YOUR QUEEN.
BONES 4 SALE

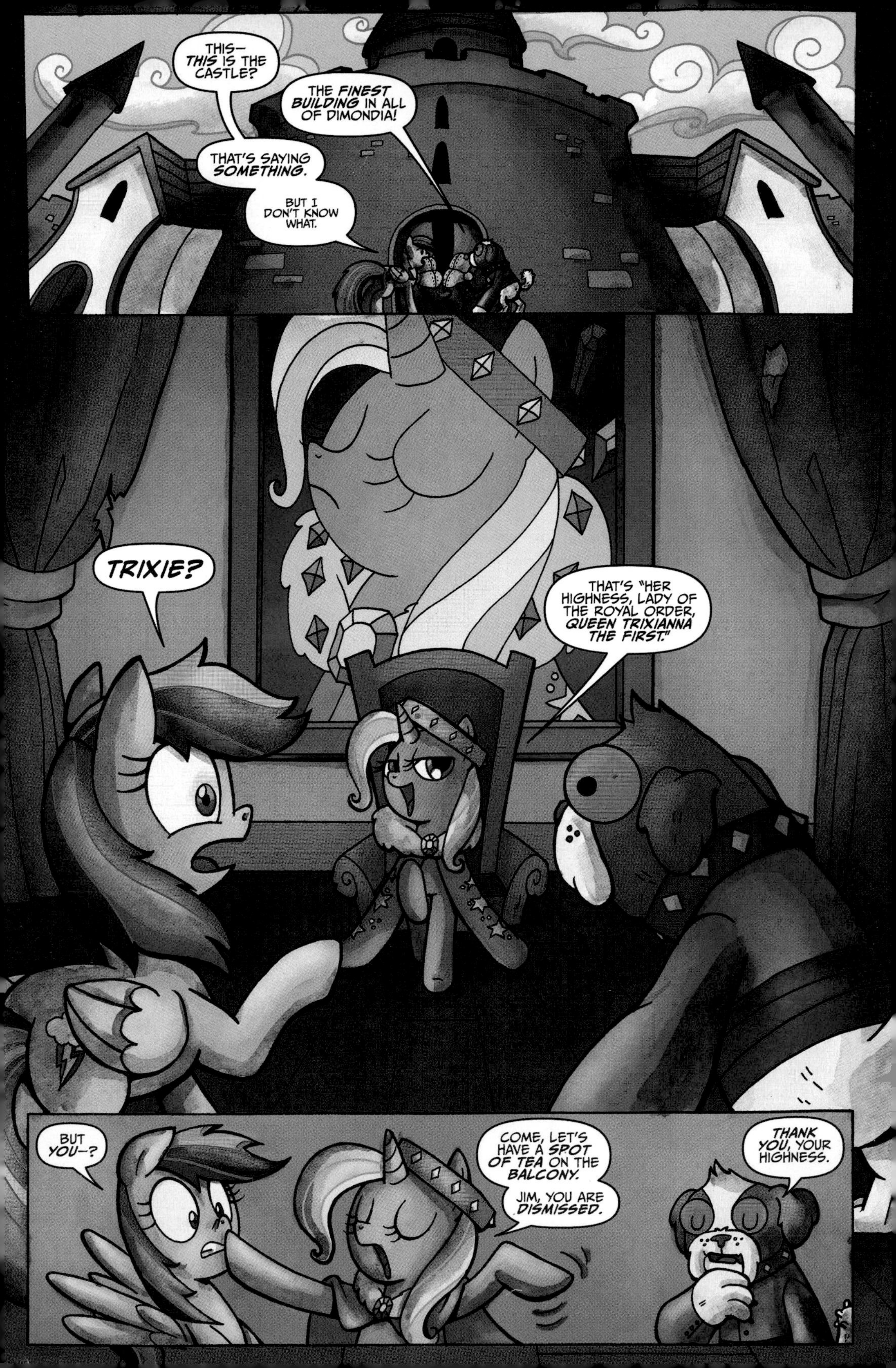

THIS—
THIS IS THE CASTLE?
THE FINEST BUILDING IN ALL OF DIMONDIA!
THAT'S SAYING SOMETHING.
BUT I DON'T KNOW WHAT.
TRIXIE?
THAT'S "HER HIGHNESS, LADY OF THE ROYAL ORDER, QUEEN TRIXIANNA THE FIRST."
BUT YOU—?
COME, LET'S HAVE A SPOT OF TEA ON THE BALCONY.
JIM, YOU ARE DISMISSED.
THANK YOU, YOUR HIGHNESS.

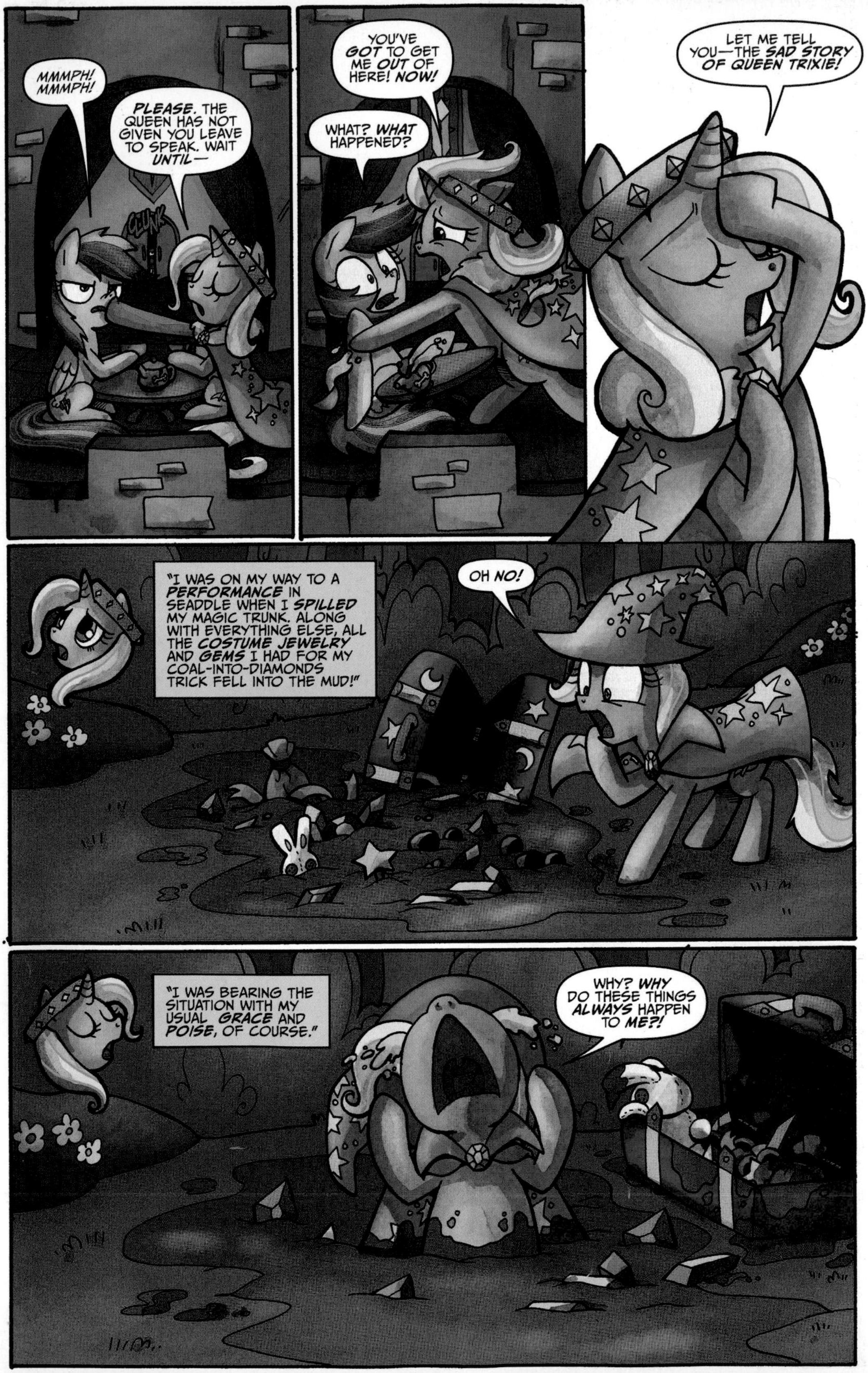
MMMPH! MMMPH!
PLEASE. THE QUEEN HAS NOT GIVEN YOU LEAVE TO SPEAK. WAIT UNTIL—
CLUNK
YOU'VE GOT TO GET ME OUT OF HERE! NOW!
WHAT? WHAT HAPPENED?
LET ME TELL YOU—THE SAD STORY OF QUEEN TRIXIE!
"I WAS ON MY WAY TO A PERFORMANCE IN SEADDLE WHEN I SPILLED MY MAGIC TRUNK. ALONG WITH EVERYTHING ELSE, ALL THE COSTUME JEWELRY AND GEMS I HAD FOR MY COAL-INTO-DIAMONDS TRICK FELL INTO THE MUD!"
OH NO!
"I WAS BEARING THE SITUATION WITH MY USUAL GRACE AND POISE, OF COURSE."
WHY? WHY DO THESE THINGS ALWAYS HAPPEN TO ME?!

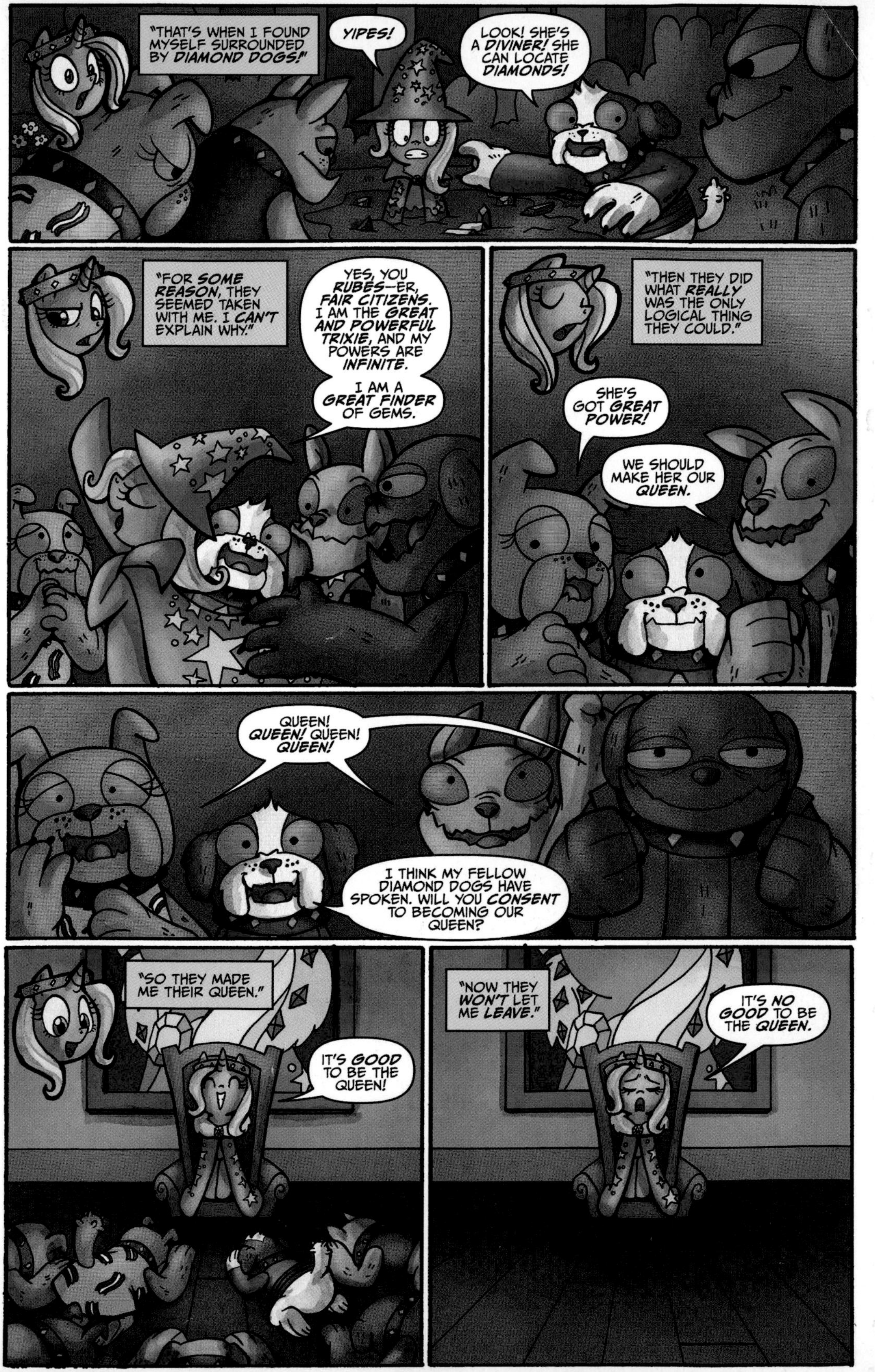
"THAT'S WHEN I FOUND MYSELF SURROUNDED BY DIAMOND DOGS!"
YIPES!
LOOK! SHE'S A DIVINER! SHE CAN LOCATE DIAMONDS!
"FOR SOME REASON, THEY SEEMED TAKEN WITH ME. I CAN'T EXPLAIN WHY."
YES, YOU RUBES—ER, FAIR CITIZENS. I AM THE GREAT AND POWERFUL TRIXIE, AND MY POWERS ARE INFINITE.
I AM A GREAT FINDER OF GEMS.
"THEN THEY DID WHAT REALLY WAS THE ONLY LOGICAL THING THEY COULD."
SHE'S GOT GREAT POWER!
WE SHOULD MAKE HER OUR QUEEN.
QUEEN! QUEEN! QUEEN! QUEEN!
I THINK MY FELLOW DIAMOND DOGS HAVE SPOKEN. WILL YOU CONSENT TO BECOMING OUR QUEEN?
"SO THEY MADE ME THEIR QUEEN."
IT'S GOOD TO BE THE QUEEN!
"NOW THEY WON'T LET ME LEAVE."
IT'S NO GOOD TO BE THE QUEEN.

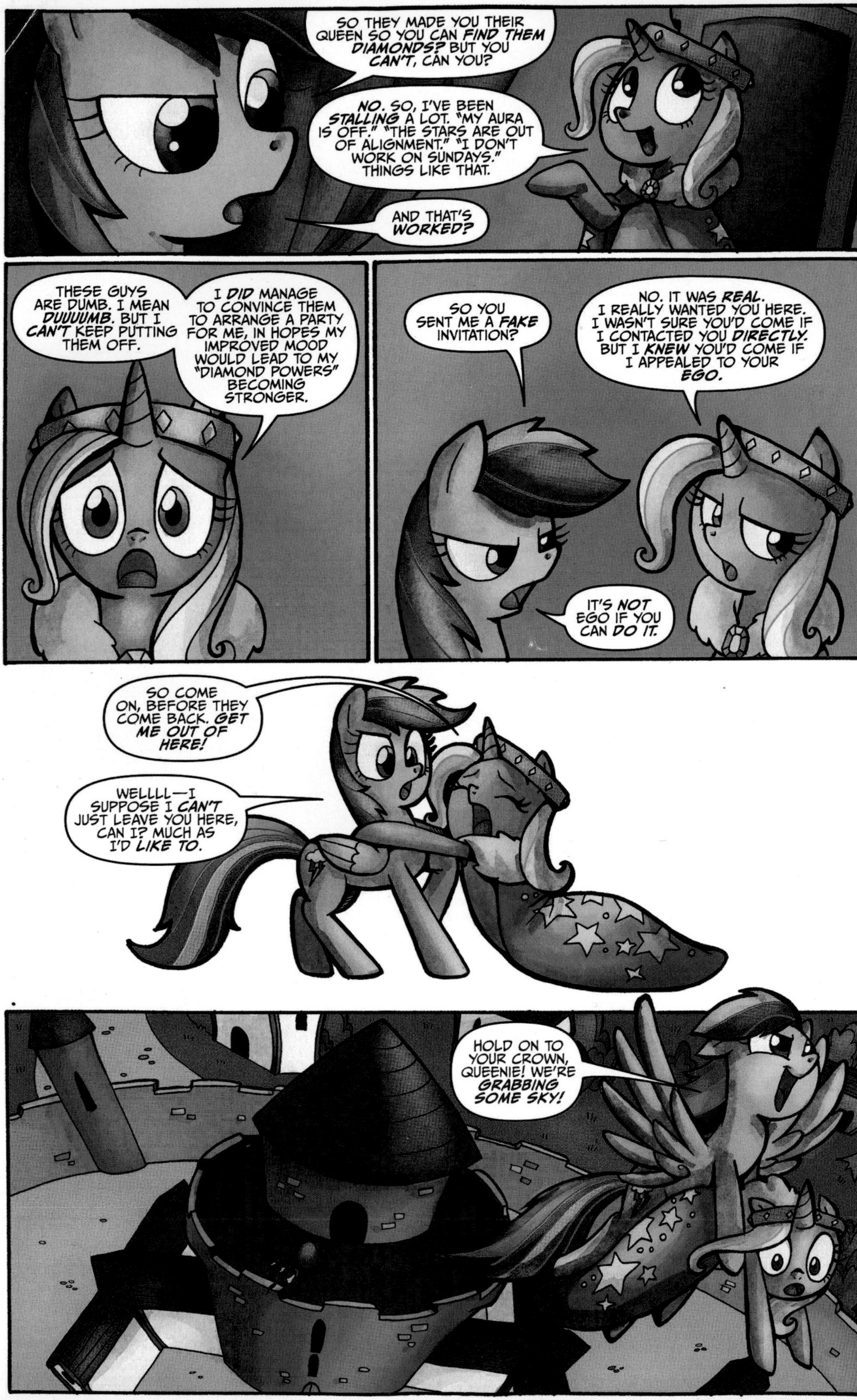
SO THEY MADE YOU THEIR QUEEN SO YOU CAN *FIND THEM DIAMONDS?* BUT YOU *CAN'T*, CAN YOU?
NO. SO, I'VE BEEN *STALLING* A LOT. "MY AURA IS OFF." "THE STARS ARE OUT OF ALIGNMENT." "I DON'T WORK ON SUNDAYS." THINGS LIKE THAT.
AND THAT'S *WORKED?*
THESE GUYS ARE DUMB. I MEAN *DUUUUMB.* BUT I *CAN'T* KEEP PUTTING THEM OFF.
I *DID* MANAGE TO CONVINCE THEM TO ARRANGE A PARTY FOR ME, IN HOPES MY IMPROVED MOOD WOULD LEAD TO MY "DIAMOND POWERS" BECOMING STRONGER.
SO YOU SENT ME A *FAKE* INVITATION?
NO. IT WAS *REAL.* I REALLY WANTED YOU HERE. I WASN'T SURE YOU'D COME IF I CONTACTED YOU *DIRECTLY.* BUT I *KNEW* YOU'D COME IF I APPEALED TO YOUR *EGO.*
IT'S *NOT* EGO IF YOU CAN *DO IT.*
SO COME ON, BEFORE THEY COME BACK. *GET ME OUT OF HERE!*
WELLLL—I SUPPOSE I *CAN'T* JUST LEAVE YOU HERE, CAN I? MUCH AS I'D *LIKE TO.*
HOLD ON TO YOUR CROWN, QUEENIE! WE'RE *GRABBING SOME SKY!*

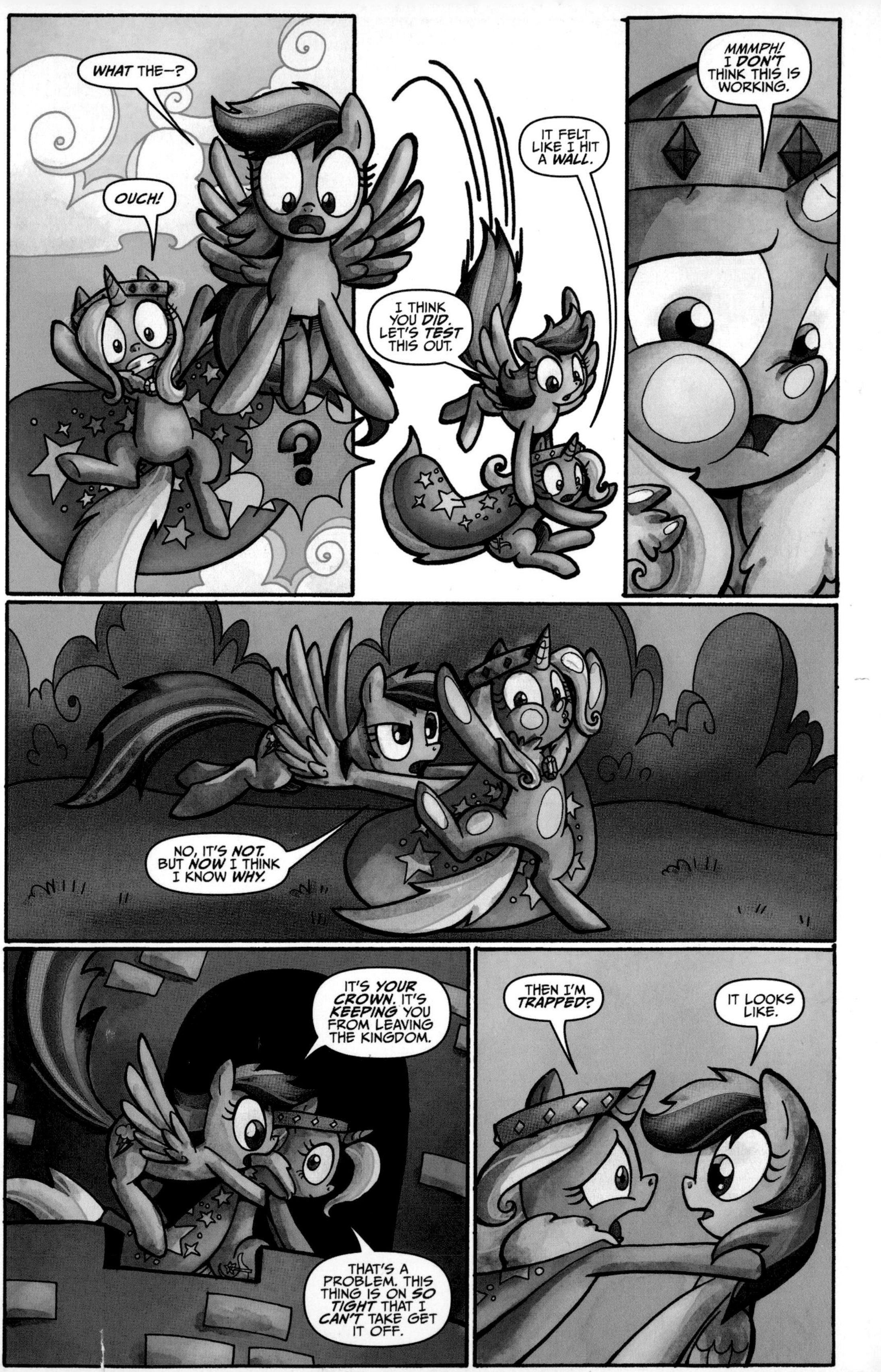
WHAT THE–?
OUCH!
IT FELT LIKE I HIT A WALL.
I THINK YOU DID. LET'S TEST THIS OUT.
MMMPH! I DON'T THINK THIS IS WORKING.
NO, IT'S NOT. BUT NOW I THINK I KNOW WHY.
IT'S YOUR CROWN. IT'S KEEPING YOU FROM LEAVING THE KINGDOM.
THAT'S A PROBLEM. THIS THING IS ON SO TIGHT THAT I CAN'T TAKE GET IT OFF.
THEN I'M TRAPPED?
IT LOOKS LIKE.

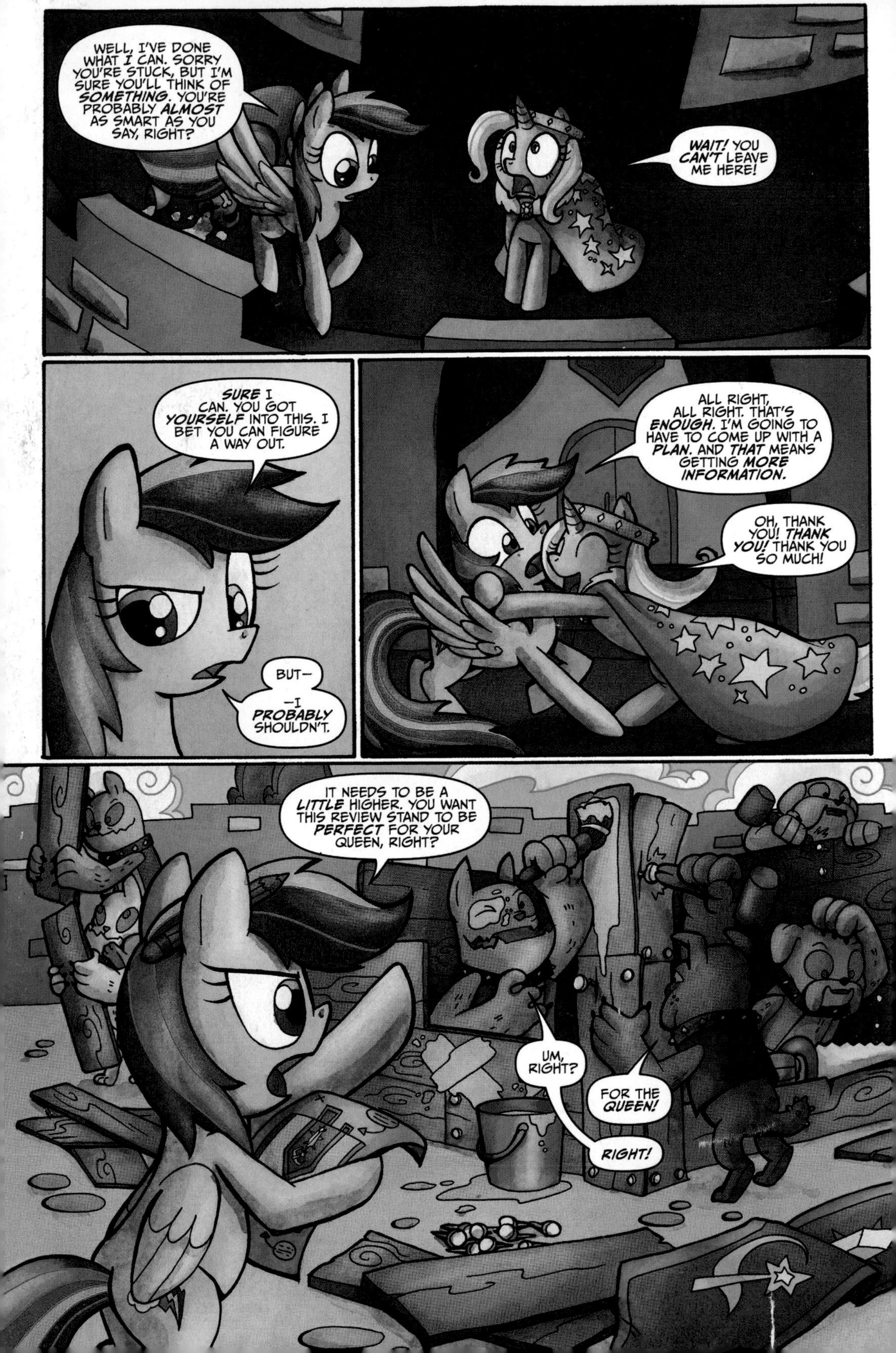
WELL, I'VE DONE WHAT *I* CAN. SORRY YOU'RE STUCK, BUT I'M SURE YOU'LL THINK OF *SOMETHING*. YOU'RE PROBABLY *ALMOST* AS SMART AS YOU SAY, RIGHT?
WAIT! YOU *CAN'T* LEAVE ME HERE!
SURE I CAN. YOU GOT *YOURSELF* INTO THIS. I BET YOU CAN FIGURE A WAY OUT.
BUT—
—I *PROBABLY* SHOULDN'T.
ALL RIGHT, ALL RIGHT. THAT'S *ENOUGH*. I'M GOING TO HAVE TO COME UP WITH A *PLAN*. AND *THAT* MEANS GETTING *MORE INFORMATION*.
OH, THANK YOU! *THANK YOU!* THANK YOU SO MUCH!
IT NEEDS TO BE A *LITTLE* HIGHER. YOU WANT THIS REVIEW STAND TO BE *PERFECT* FOR YOUR QUEEN, RIGHT?
UM, RIGHT?
FOR THE *QUEEN!*
RIGHT!

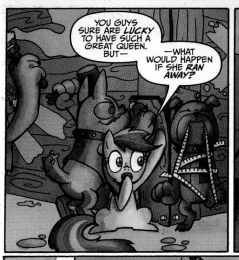

YOU GUYS SURE ARE *LUCKY* TO HAVE SUCH A GREAT QUEEN. BUT—

—WHAT WOULD HAPPEN IF SHE *RAN AWAY?*

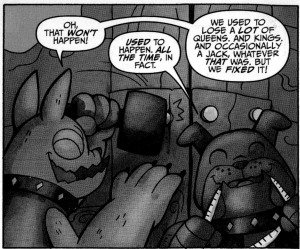

OH, THAT *WON'T* HAPPEN!

USED TO HAPPEN. *ALL THE TIME,* IN FACT.

WE USED TO LOSE A *LOT* OF QUEENS. AND KINGS. AND OCCASIONALLY A JACK, WHATEVER *THAT* WAS. BUT WE *FIXED* IT!

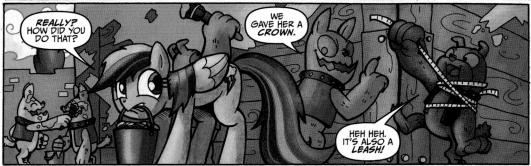

REALLY? HOW DID YOU DO THAT?

WE GAVE HER A *CROWN.*

HEH HEH. IT'S ALSO A *LEASH!*

THE CROWN IS *MAGIC.* IT WON'T LET HER LEAVE THE CITY WHILE SHE WEARS IT. AND SHE *CAN'T* TAKE IT OFF.

EVER?

NOPE. *NEVER.*

WELL—

—UNLESS WE DIAMOND DOGS START TO *LOSE FAITH* IN HER AS OUR QUEEN. *TRUE* EXECUTIVE POWER IS, OF COURSE, DERIVED FROM THE PEOPLE. A CHIEF EXECUTIVE SERVES AT THE *PLEASURE* OF THE *ELECTORATE.*

THAT'S *VERY* INTERESTING.

WHAT? I READ IT SOMEWHERE!

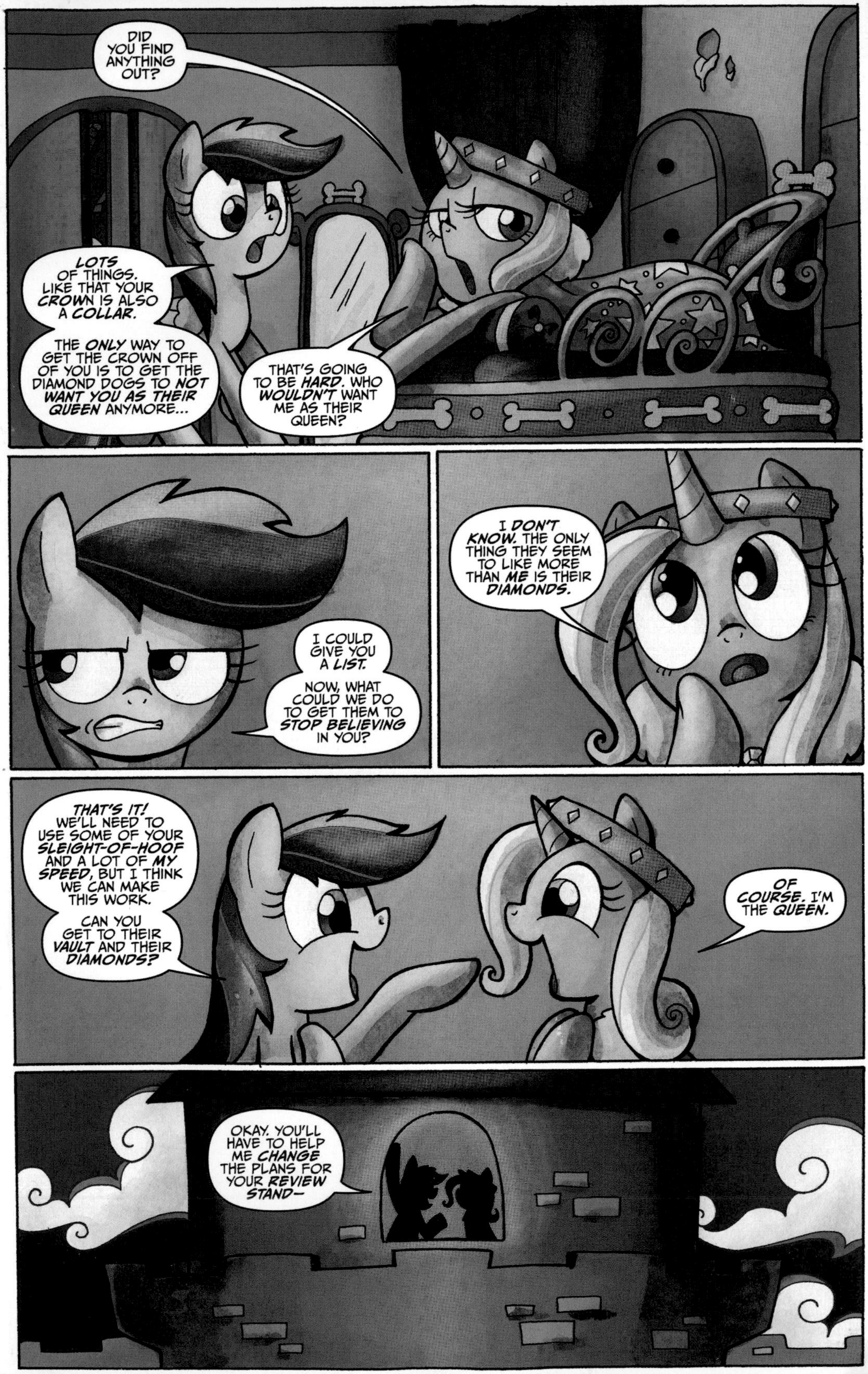
DID YOU FIND ANYTHING OUT?
LOTS OF THINGS. LIKE THAT YOUR CROWN IS ALSO A COLLAR.
THE ONLY WAY TO GET THE CROWN OFF OF YOU IS TO GET THE DIAMOND DOGS TO NOT WANT YOU AS THEIR QUEEN ANYMORE...
THAT'S GOING TO BE HARD. WHO WOULDN'T WANT ME AS THEIR QUEEN?
I COULD GIVE YOU A LIST.
NOW, WHAT COULD WE DO TO GET THEM TO STOP BELIEVING IN YOU?
I DON'T KNOW. THE ONLY THING THEY SEEM TO LIKE MORE THAN ME IS THEIR DIAMONDS.
THAT'S IT! WE'LL NEED TO USE SOME OF YOUR SLEIGHT-OF-HOOF AND A LOT OF MY SPEED, BUT I THINK WE CAN MAKE THIS WORK.
CAN YOU GET TO THEIR VAULT AND THEIR DIAMONDS?
OF COURSE. I'M THE QUEEN.
OKAY. YOU'LL HAVE TO HELP ME CHANGE THE PLANS FOR YOUR REVIEW STAND—

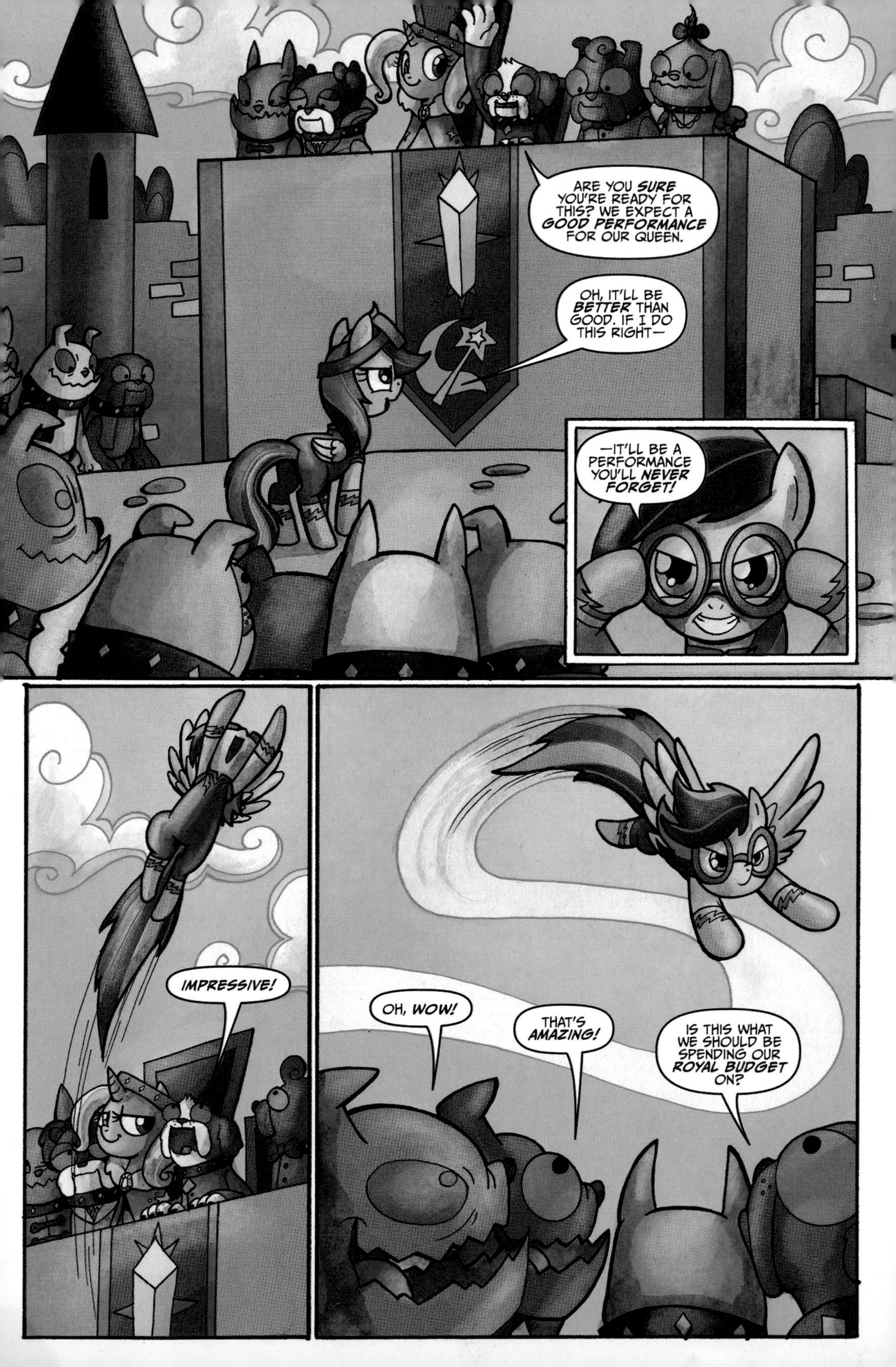
ARE YOU SURE YOU'RE READY FOR THIS? WE EXPECT A GOOD PERFORMANCE FOR OUR QUEEN.
OH, IT'LL BE BETTER THAN GOOD. IF I DO THIS RIGHT—
—IT'LL BE A PERFORMANCE YOU'LL NEVER FORGET!
IMPRESSIVE!
OH, WOW!
THAT'S AMAZING!
IS THIS WHAT WE SHOULD BE SPENDING OUR ROYAL BUDGET ON?

SHE IS *FANTASTIC*, MY QUEEN!

YES, INDEED. I'VE NEVER SEEN *ANYTHING* LIKE THIS.

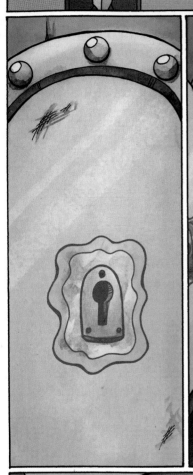

OH MY! THAT LOOKS *HARD.*

YOU HAVE *NO IDEA.*

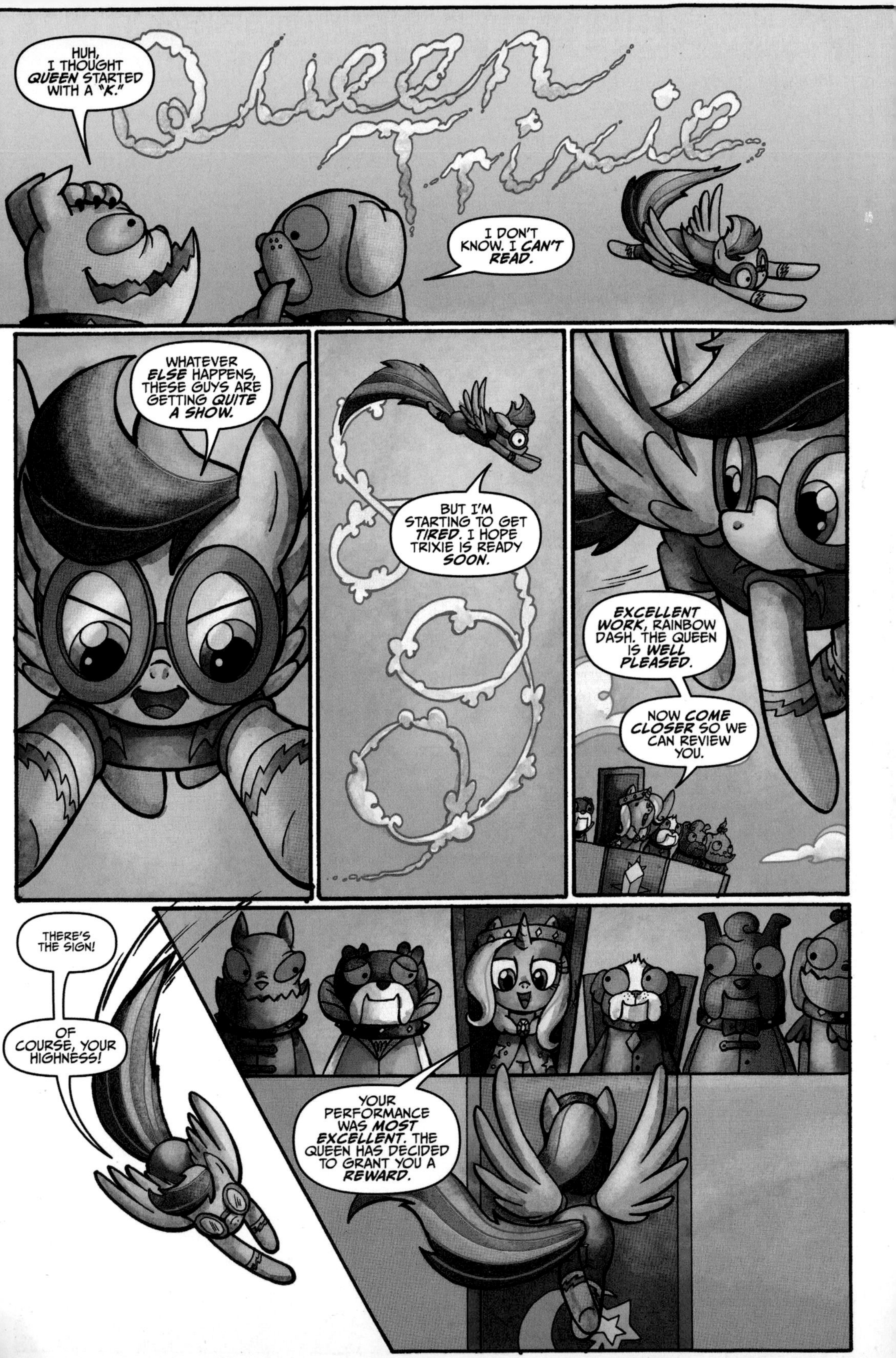
HUH, I THOUGHT QUEEN STARTED WITH A "K."
Queen Trixie
I DON'T KNOW. I CAN'T READ.
WHATEVER ELSE HAPPENS, THESE GUYS ARE GETTING QUITE A SHOW.
BUT I'M STARTING TO GET TIRED. I HOPE TRIXIE IS READY SOON.
EXCELLENT WORK, RAINBOW DASH. THE QUEEN IS WELL PLEASED.
NOW COME CLOSER SO WE CAN REVIEW YOU.
THERE'S THE SIGN!
OF COURSE, YOUR HIGHNESS!
YOUR PERFORMANCE WAS MOST EXCELLENT. THE QUEEN HAS DECIDED TO GRANT YOU A REWARD.

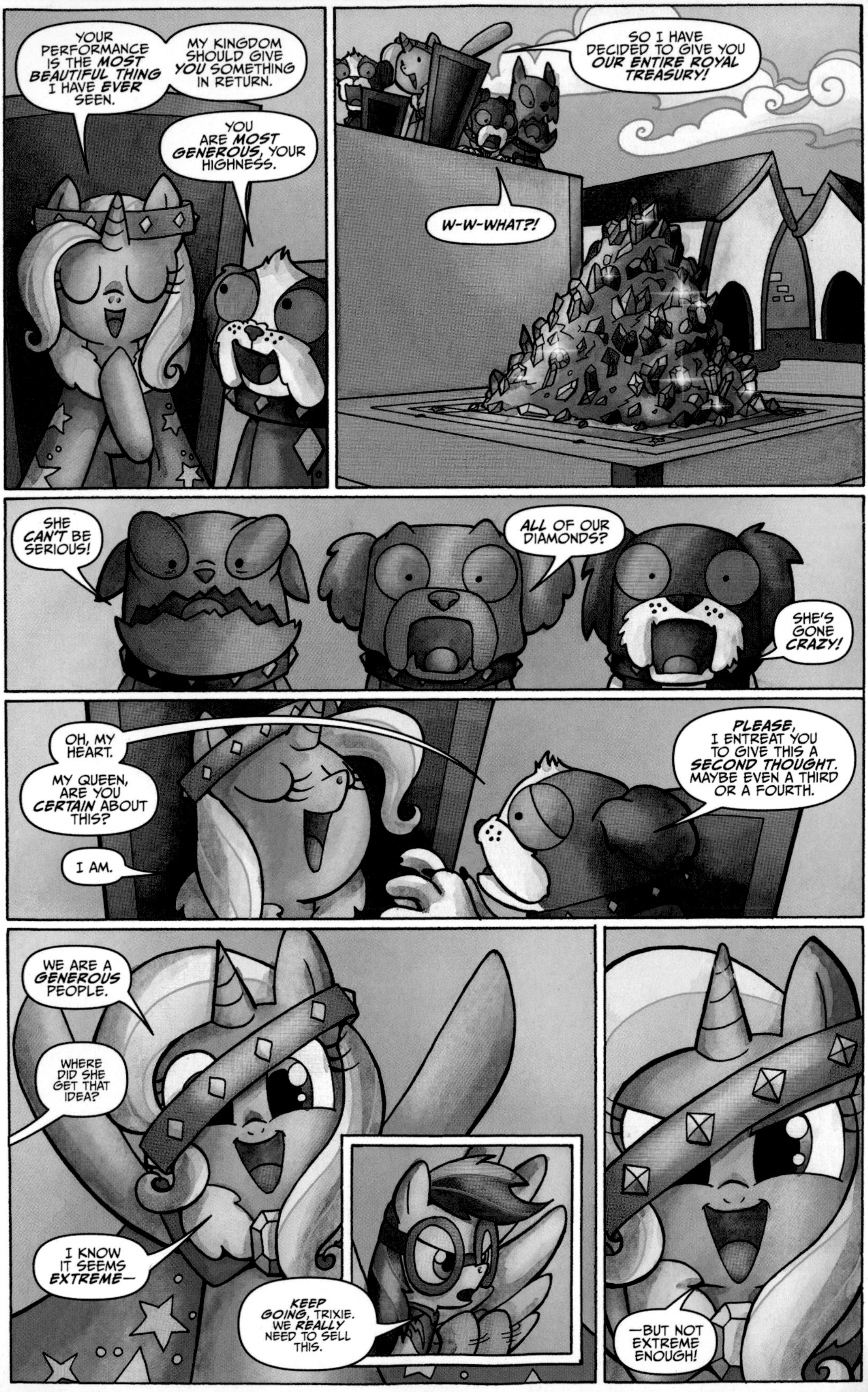
YOUR PERFORMANCE IS THE MOST BEAUTIFUL THING I HAVE EVER SEEN.
MY KINGDOM SHOULD GIVE YOU SOMETHING IN RETURN.
YOU ARE MOST GENEROUS, YOUR HIGHNESS.
SO I HAVE DECIDED TO GIVE YOU OUR ENTIRE ROYAL TREASURY!
W-W-WHAT?!
SHE CAN'T BE SERIOUS!
ALL OF OUR DIAMONDS?
SHE'S GONE CRAZY!
OH, MY HEART.
MY QUEEN, ARE YOU CERTAIN ABOUT THIS?
I AM.
PLEASE, I ENTREAT YOU TO GIVE THIS A SECOND THOUGHT. MAYBE EVEN A THIRD OR A FOURTH.
WE ARE A GENEROUS PEOPLE.
WHERE DID SHE GET THAT IDEA?
I KNOW IT SEEMS EXTREME—
KEEP GOING, TRIXIE. WE REALLY NEED TO SELL THIS.
—BUT NOT EXTREME ENOUGH!

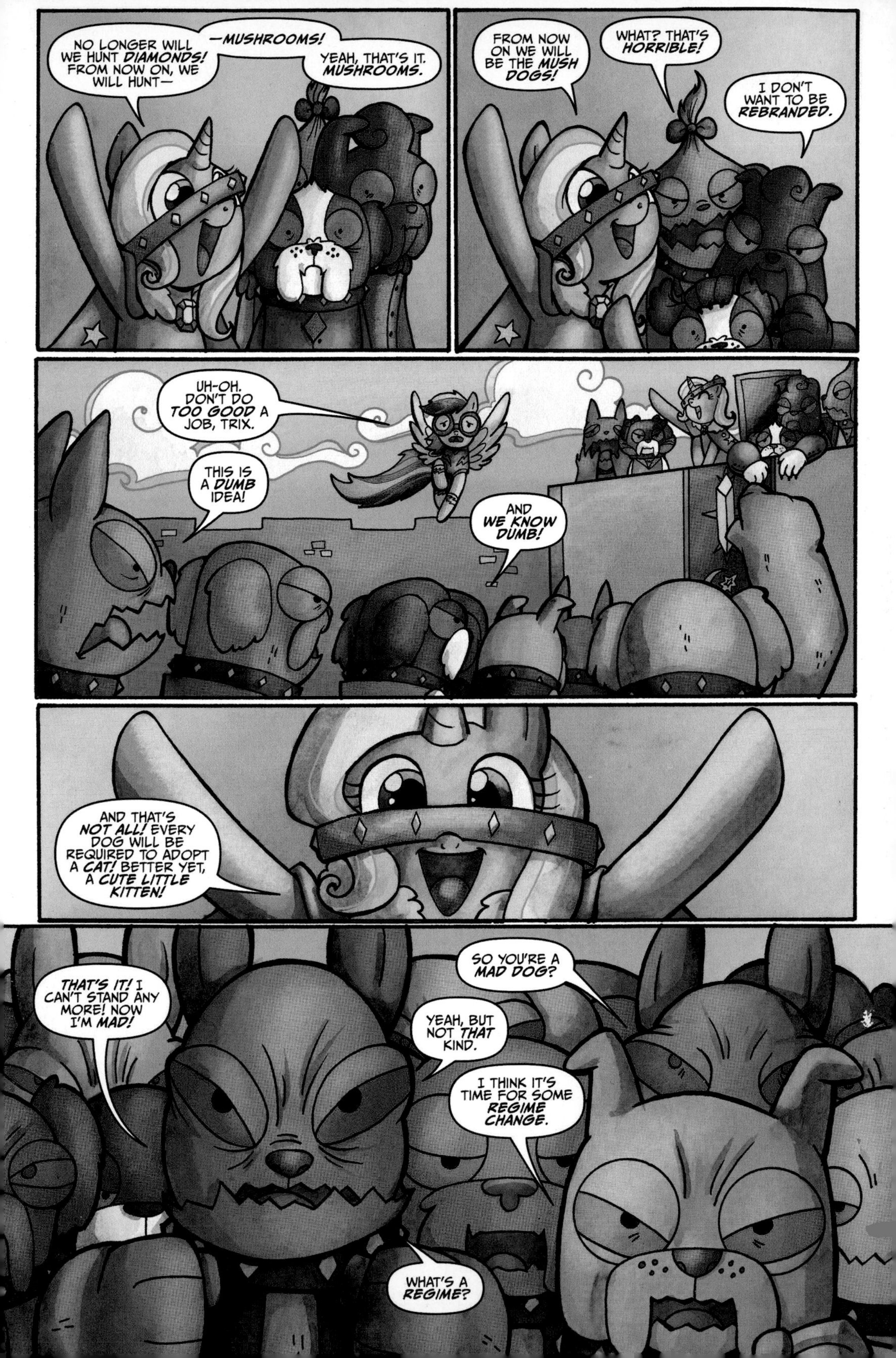
NO LONGER WILL WE HUNT *DIAMONDS!* FROM NOW ON, WE WILL HUNT—
—*MUSHROOMS!*
YEAH, THAT'S IT. *MUSHROOMS.*
FROM NOW ON WE WILL BE THE *MUSH DOGS!*
WHAT? THAT'S *HORRIBLE!*
I DON'T WANT TO BE *REBRANDED.*
UH-OH. DON'T DO *TOO GOOD* A JOB, TRIX.
THIS IS A *DUMB* IDEA!
AND *WE KNOW DUMB!*
AND THAT'S *NOT ALL!* EVERY DOG WILL BE REQUIRED TO ADOPT A *CAT!* BETTER YET, A *CUTE LITTLE KITTEN!*
THAT'S IT! I CAN'T STAND ANY MORE! NOW I'M *MAD!*
SO YOU'RE A *MAD DOG?*
YEAH, BUT NOT *THAT* KIND.
I THINK IT'S TIME FOR SOME *REGIME CHANGE.*
WHAT'S A *REGIME?*

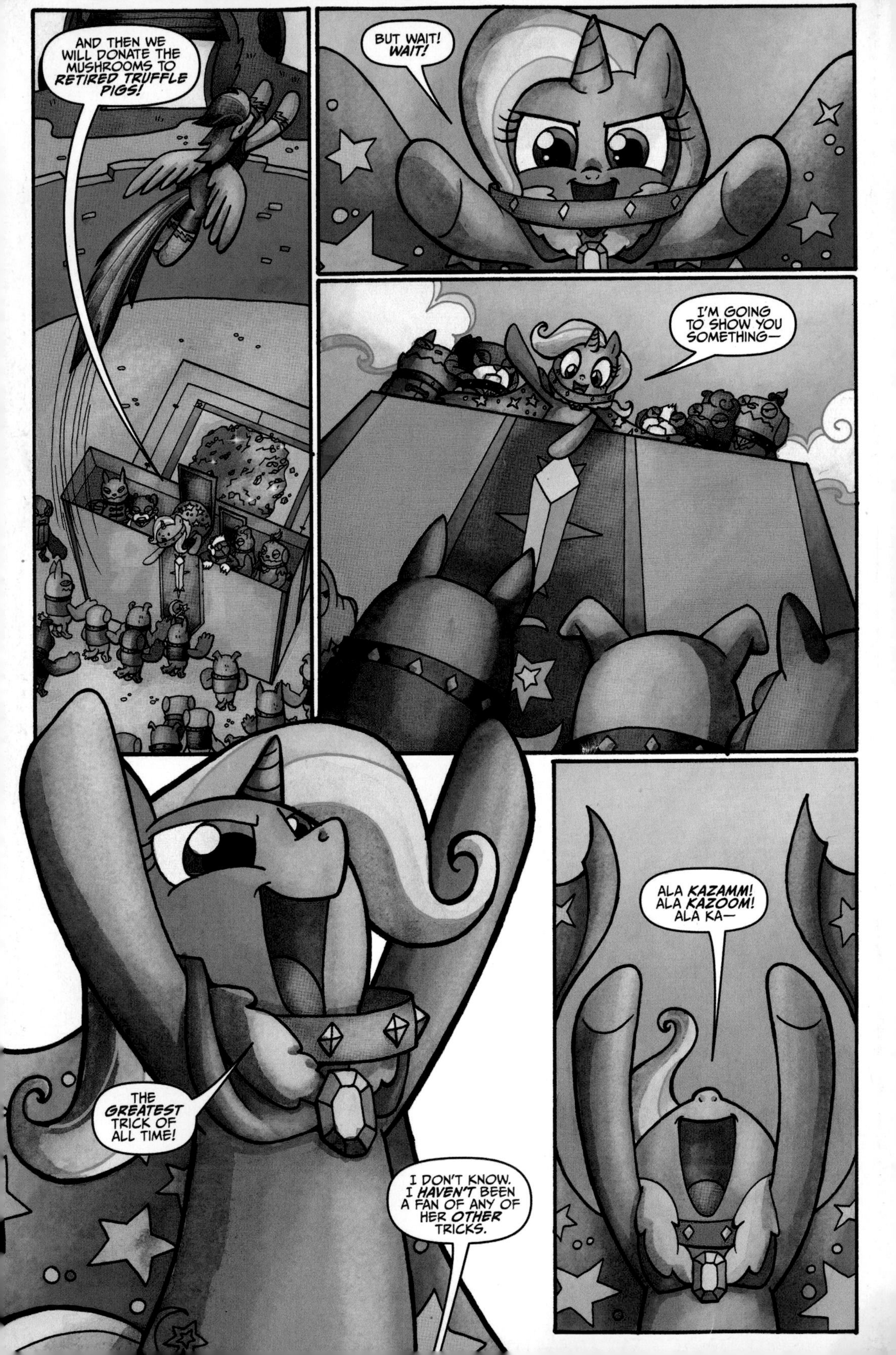
AND THEN WE WILL DONATE THE MUSHROOMS TO RETIRED TRUFFLE PIGS!
BUT WAIT! WAIT!
I'M GOING TO SHOW YOU SOMETHING—
THE GREATEST TRICK OF ALL TIME!
I DON'T KNOW. I HAVEN'T BEEN A FAN OF ANY OF HER OTHER TRICKS.
ALA KAZAMM! ALA KAZOOM! ALA KA—

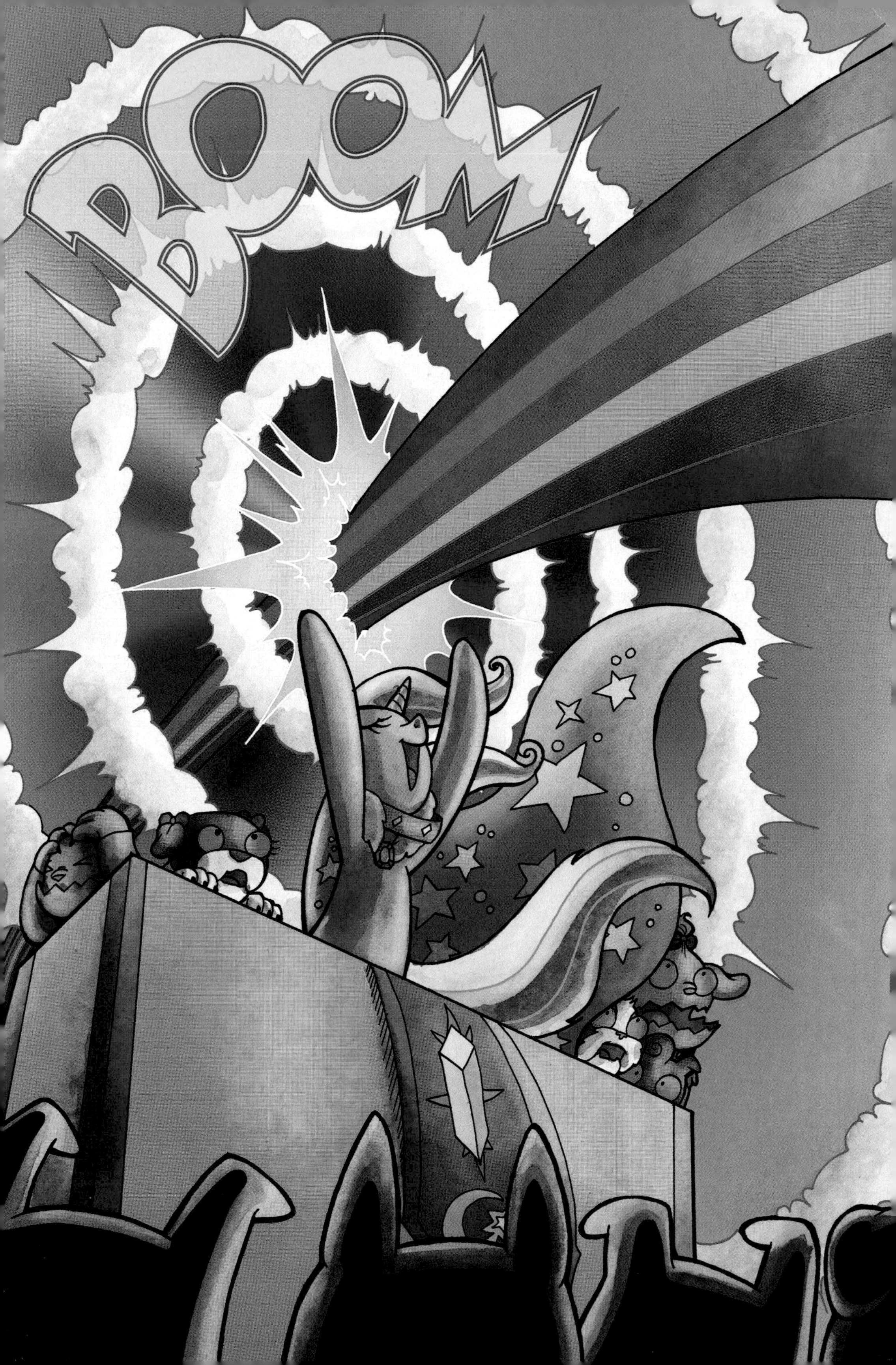
BOOM

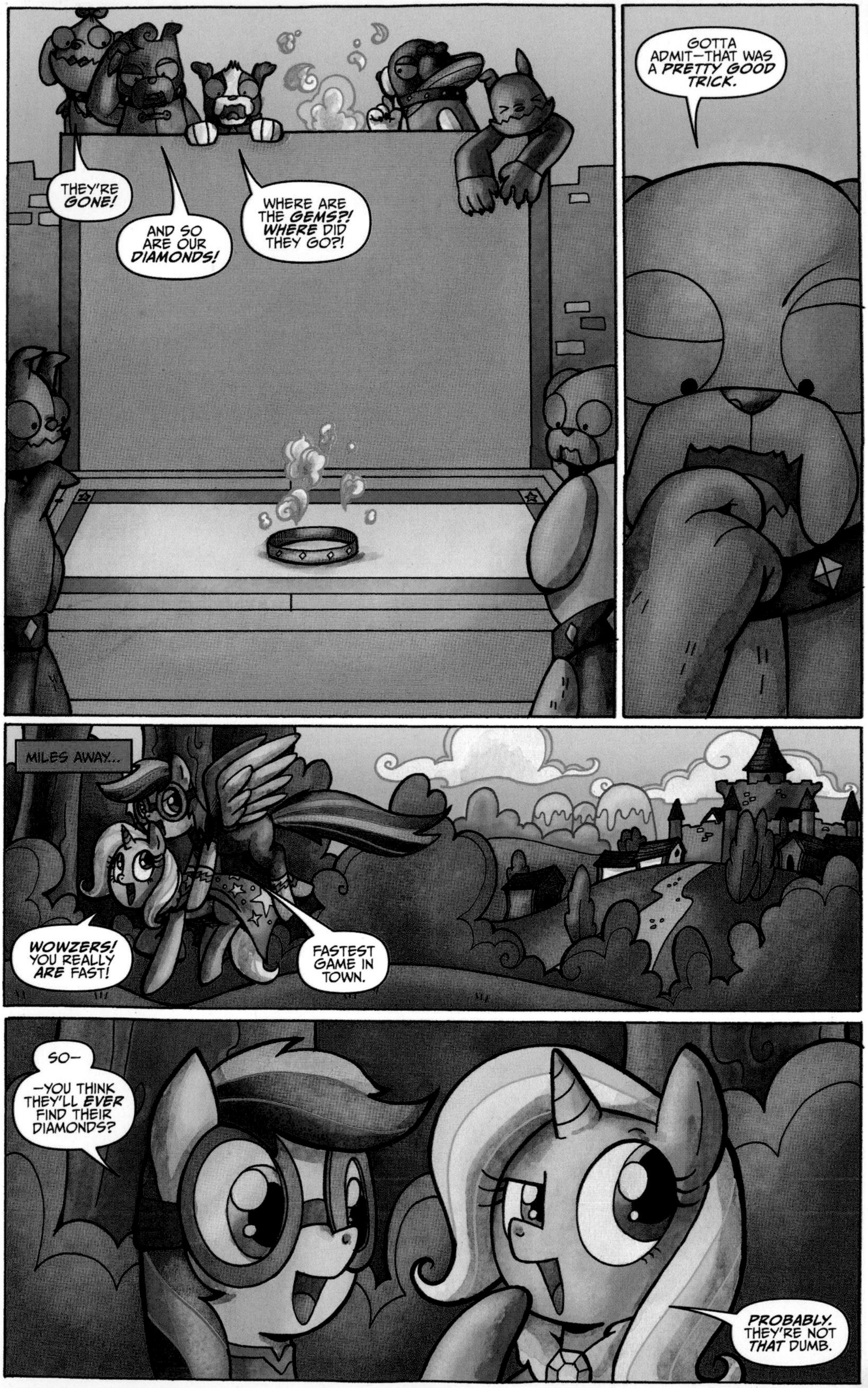
THEY'RE *GONE!*
AND SO ARE OUR *DIAMONDS!*
WHERE ARE THE *GEMS?! WHERE* DID THEY GO?!
GOTTA ADMIT—THAT WAS A *PRETTY GOOD TRICK.*
MILES AWAY...
WOWZERS! YOU REALLY *ARE* FAST!
FASTEST GAME IN TOWN.
SO—
—YOU THINK THEY'LL *EVER* FIND THEIR DIAMONDS?
PROBABLY. THEY'RE NOT *THAT* DUMB.

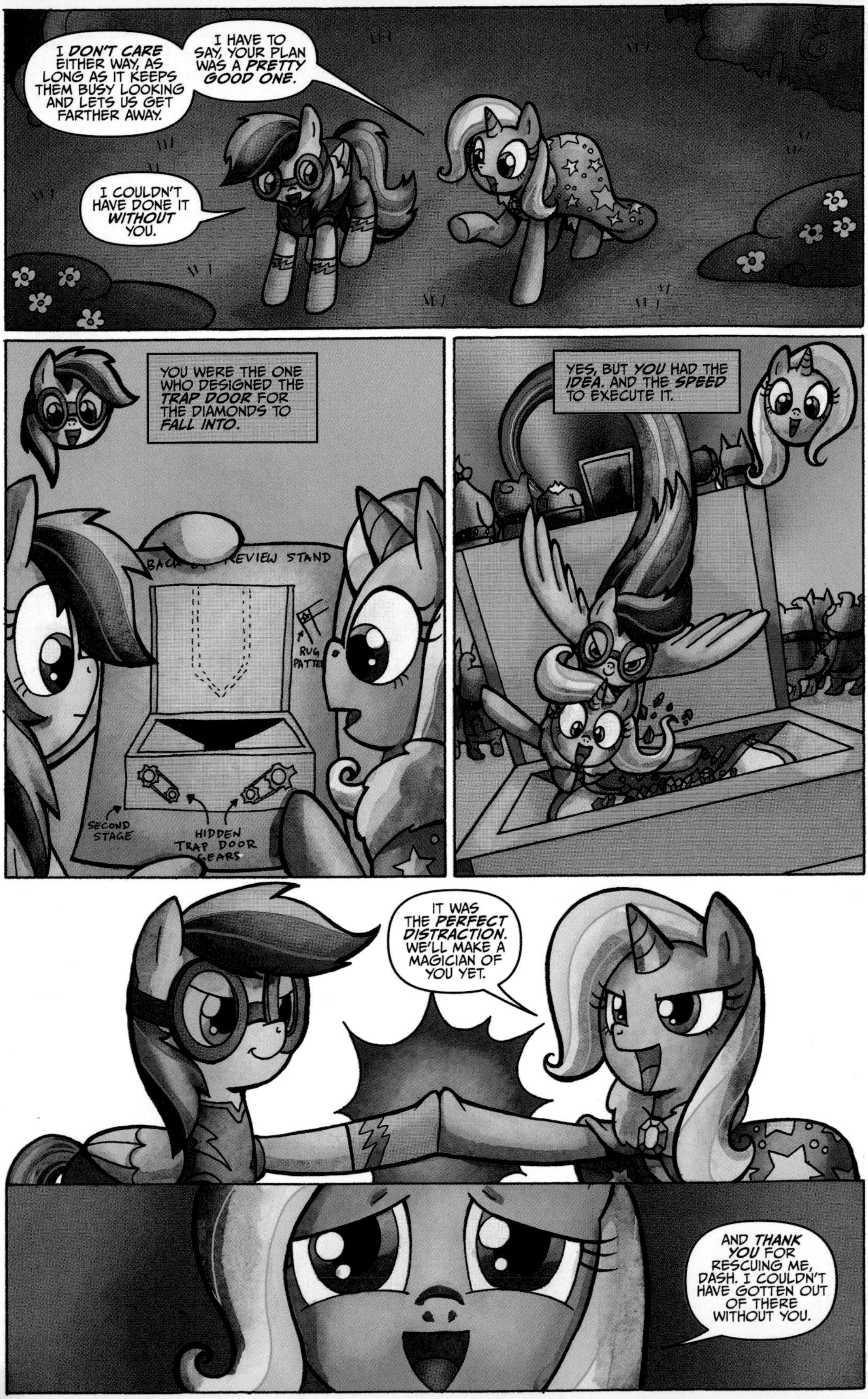

I DON'T CARE EITHER WAY, AS LONG AS IT KEEPS THEM BUSY LOOKING AND LETS US GET FARTHER AWAY.
I HAVE TO SAY, YOUR PLAN WAS A PRETTY GOOD ONE.
I COULDN'T HAVE DONE IT WITHOUT YOU.
YOU WERE THE ONE WHO DESIGNED THE TRAP DOOR FOR THE DIAMONDS TO FALL INTO.
REVIEW STAND
RUG
SECOND STAGE
HIDDEN TRAP DOOR
YES, BUT YOU HAD THE IDEA. AND THE SPEED TO EXECUTE IT.
IT WAS THE PERFECT DISTRACTION. WE'LL MAKE A MAGICIAN OF YOU YET.
AND THANK YOU FOR RESCUING ME, DASH. I COULDN'T HAVE GOTTEN OUT OF THERE WITHOUT YOU.

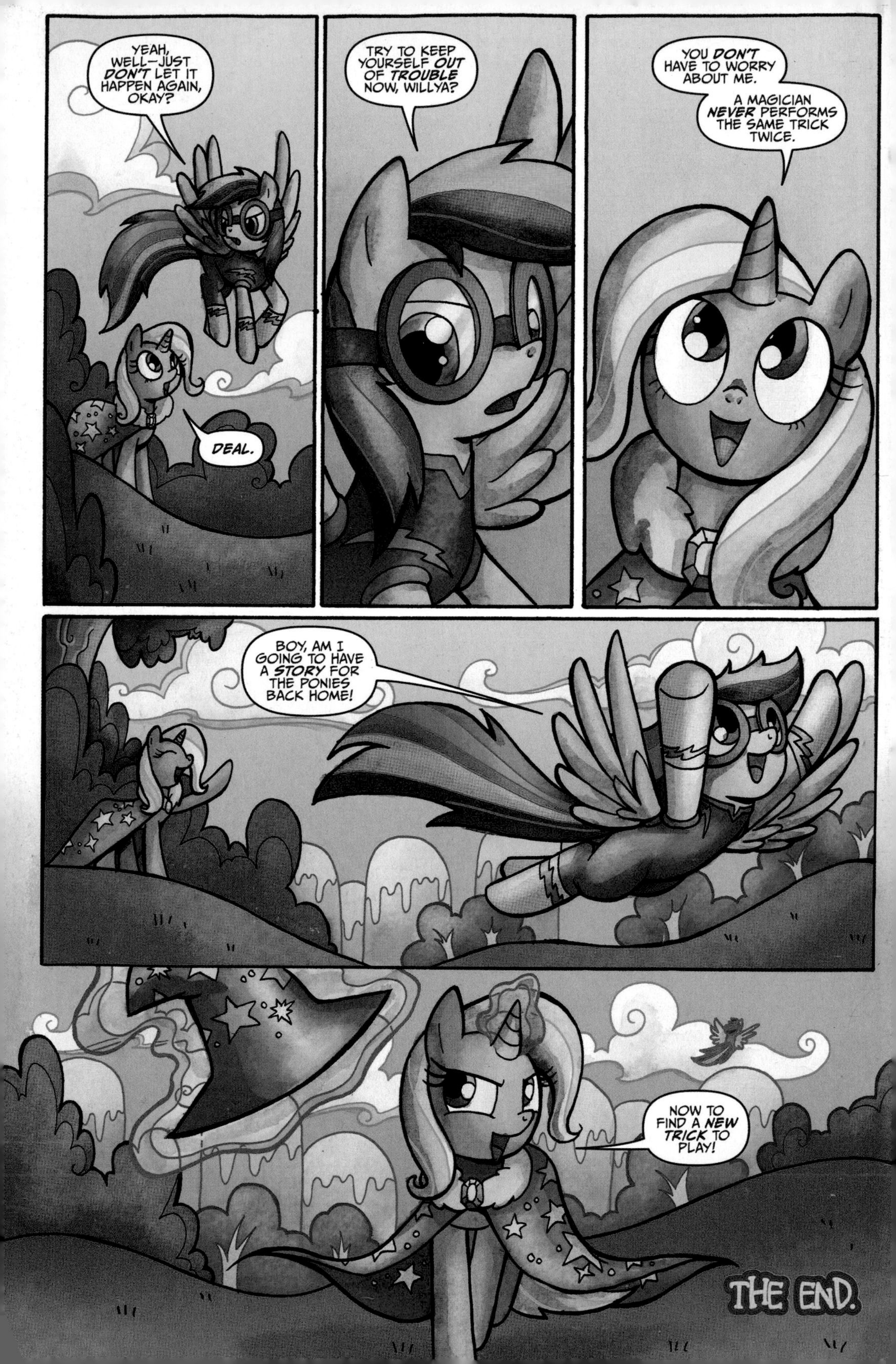
YEAH, WELL—JUST DON'T LET IT HAPPEN AGAIN, OKAY?
DEAL.
TRY TO KEEP YOURSELF OUT OF TROUBLE NOW, WILLYA?
YOU DON'T HAVE TO WORRY ABOUT ME.
A MAGICIAN NEVER PERFORMS THE SAME TRICK TWICE.
BOY, AM I GOING TO HAVE A STORY FOR THE PONIES BACK HOME!
NOW TO FIND A NEW TRICK TO PLAY!
THE END.

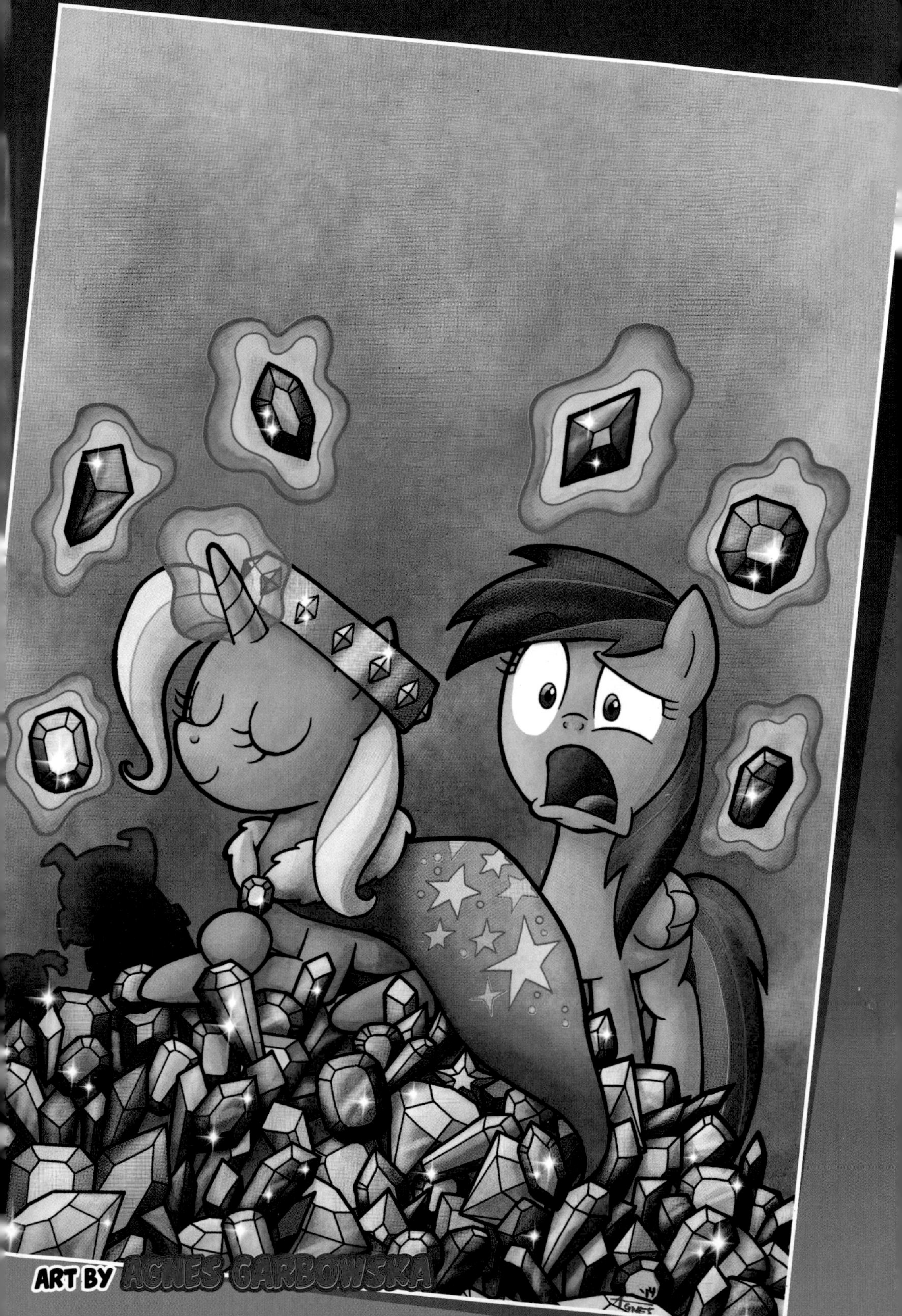

ART BY AGNES GARBOWSKA

These collections on sale now!

My Little Pony: Friendship Is Magic, Vol. 1
ISBN: 978-1-61377-605-6

My Little Pony: Pony Tales, Vol. 1
ISBN: 978-1-61377-740-4

My Little Pony: The Magic Begins
ISBN: 978-1-61377-754-1

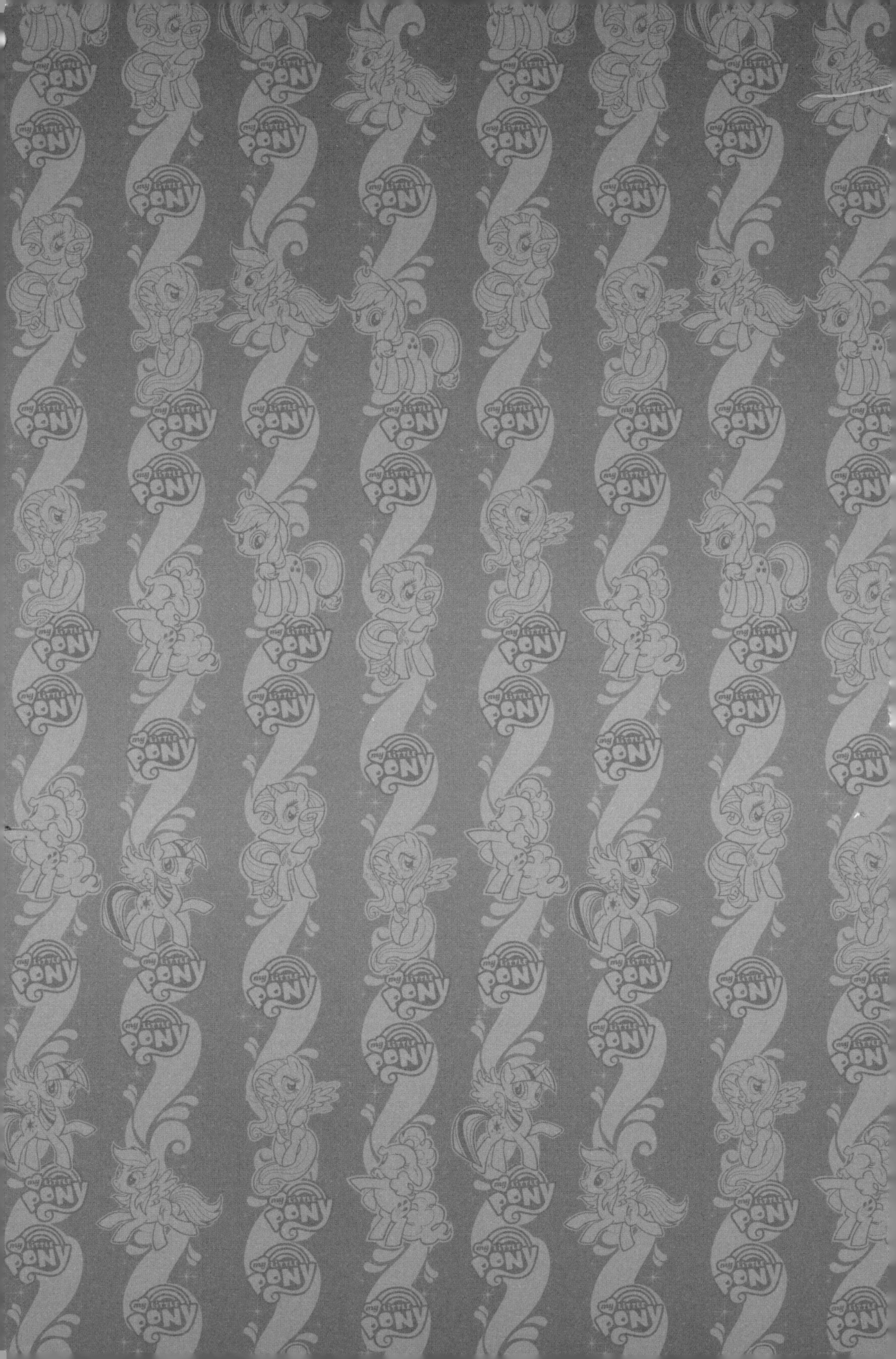
my little PONY